MON

SHERIFF
LUKE LUDD

Other books by D.J. Bishop:

Showdown at Deer Creek
Luke Ludd

SHERIFF LUKE LUDD

•

D.J. Bishop

AVALON BOOKS
NEW YORK

Published by Thomas Bouregy & Co., Inc.
160 Madison Avenue, New York, NY 10016

Library of Congress Cataloging-in-Publication Data

Bishop, D.J.
    Sheriff Luke Ludd / by D.J. Bishop
      p.   cm.
    ISBN 0-8034-9791-1 (acid-free paper)
  1. Sheriffs—Fiction.   I. Title.

    PS3602.I756S47   2006
    813'.6—dc22

                  2005037654

PRINTED IN THE UNITED STATES OF AMERICA
ON ACID-FREE PAPER
BY HADDON CRAFTSMEN, BLOOMSBURG, PENNSYLVANIA

Grateful Appreciation To:

Carolyn Lea

Without her love and support this would be a
very sad and lonely world.

Guy and Mary Lea Randall

My number one fans whose faith in my story telling got
me started and kept me going.

L. W. (Jack) and Claudie May (Dollie) Bishop

Two great people who lived it.

A Special Thanks To:

Blanche Jamison

Without her friendship and help in editing, this book
would have never been published.

And To:

Virginia, Effie, Mary, Claude, Judy, Kelly, Jackie, Estelle, Donnie
Joe, Joe Lee, Jay, Dillon, Rocky, and Denise because without their
inspiration the story would have never been told. And a very
special thanks to my twin brother Tommie G. Bishop, because a
day without him in it would be a very dark and lonely day . . . it
would be a day of no light and no sound.

And Let's Not Forget:

All the many true cowboys I've had the pleasure of knowing in
my life. May the ones still with us always be mounted fresh and
ride where the prairie is wide, the air clean, and the water cool
and clear. And to the many who have already rode over the
distant horizon and faded into the sunset, may they always be
remembered in a good light and where ever they are,
may they rest in peace.

D.J. Bishop
http://www.authordjbishop.com

In memory of
Major Guy G Randall USAFR, my number one fan and a good friend.
A finer man I never met.

Chapter One

The sun was starting to set on the western horizon, its reddish-orange rays, like long blades of grass, streaking the light-blue, hazy sky; and with each passing moment its bright glow was fading. As darkness quickly approached, Luke rode on knowing once the light of day was gone the killer he sought would have the upper hand. He knew Pots Logan could sit with his gun at the ready, watching his back trail until Luke rode into view. Judging by the freshness of the marks, Pots could not be far ahead; Luke knew he was steadily closing in. Despite the danger he rode through the dim light along a dry creek bottom, one eye on the ground looking for signs, the other watching the trail ahead.

Luke Ludd tracked with his mind as well as his senses. As his eyes read the trail, his mind leaped ahead to the purpose and destination of the man or men he tracked.

A tall, lean man with quiet ways, Luke was a man of few words, and when he spoke folks did well to listen. Once he accepted a challenge he would see it through no matter what. He stood well over six feet, with a muscular frame, wide, powerful shoulders, and a solid chest that tapered to a small waist. His face was leathery brown from the sun and wind, with a thick, coal-black, drooping mustache covering much of his mouth. He had a full head of neatly-trimmed hair of the same color.

He was considered a handsome man and his rugged good looks brought long stares from women young and old alike. Yet his mere presence could send fear through the hearts and minds of his enemies.

Luke suddenly noticed something move in the trees ahead. It was not a big movement, but enough to catch his eye not near the ground but higher up in the branches. He drew up hoping to see the movement again, and when he did, realized it was a wisp of smoke. Pots Logan had made a bad mistake—one that would probably cost him his life. He had stopped and made camp.

Luke quietly stepped to the ground. After tying Mousy to a low limb, he slipped his Winchester from its boot. He worked the action slowly, forcing a bullet deep into the chamber. With his rifle ready, Luke reached down and slipped the leather thong from over the hammer of his Colt. He began moving through the underbrush in the direction of the rising smoke. He advanced slowly, hunkered down, moving one foot at a time. At a massive oak, he paused in the cover of its low branches, and stood holding his breath, listening. The only sound to be heard was the uneven pounding of his own beating heart.

Luke started from under the tree but had taken only a couple of steps when his instincts suddenly told him to stop. He stood perfectly still, his eyes searching the ever-growing darkness, his ears straining to hear, but saw and heard nothing. Trusting the instincts that had kept him alive over the years, he studied the situation a while longer, unsure of what his mind was trying to tell him. Slowly he dropped to his hands and knees and started to crawl. As he worked his way through the thick, tangled, sometimes thorny brush he cleared the ground of all dry leaves and sticks before he put down a hand, and he was just as careful to place each knee in the same place he had just picked up a hand.

Coming to a little ridge, Luke stretched out and lay flat on his belly, then slowly parted a clump of tall prairie grass with the barrel of his rifle and looked through. No more than ten yards away a man sat on a large, flat rock sipping coffee in the flickering glow of a small campfire.

He was a big man with broad heavy shoulders, powerful arms, and large hands. He wore a six-gun slung low and tied to his leg. The sight of Pots Logan made his pulse quicken and the hair on the back of his neck stiffen. He tightened his grip on the stock of the Winchester and moved his finger over the trigger. He knew that Pots, like his brother Leonard, would never be taken alive. It was only a matter of time before this Logan would also be dead.

Pots pitched wood on the fire and the flames leaped high into the air, lighting up the outlaw's heavily-bearded face and revealing a man tired and hungry—too tired to run any further, but hungry enough to stand and fight. The man slowly sipped at his coffee unaware of the present danger. Or was he?

Over the past three weeks Luke had come to know this man well, and possibly better than Pots Logan knew himself.

He was a proven cold-blooded killer, of how many Luke was not certain though he was sure of two. Both deaths had been as senseless as any he had seen since he and the Langtrys had cleaned Maxwell Laughlin and that bunch out of Rising Star and by far the worst since Luke had become the town sheriff just a little over a year ago. He had stopped by the Tidwell farm just to visit when he made the awful discovery.

Tom Tidwell and his lovely wife Beth had been well along in years and fine, decent, hardworking people with hearts as big as the Texas sky. They had been good friends to Luke's father, Luther Ludd, right up until his death, and Luke had known them all his life. Together they had owned and worked a small dirt farm on the east fork of Dead Cow Creek where they raised vegetables of all kinds in their garden. From that fine garden most of the town folk got what they needed each spring and summer, for their tables and to put up in jars for the winter.

They had each died quickly with a single gunshot to the head. Every room of their old house had been ransacked, and the pockets of Tom's old, ragged overalls were turned inside out. The four old mules and the wagon were missing from the barn and Luke had followed the deep wagon ruts northwest to Abilene. There he learned that the wagon and mules had been sold, just a week earlier, to the man at the livery for less than half what they were worth.

From there the trail headed west to Sweetwater where Luke learned from Sheriff Carl Padgett that the two men he was tracking were most likely brothers by the name of Pots and Leonard Logan. There were three more brothers, Billy, Kirk, and Sid, and all five had grown up in a little run-down, two-room shack just a few miles south of town.

Their mother, Rachel Logan, a beautiful, high-spirited woman, had run off fifteen years back with a gambler passing through on his way to the mining camps up north.

Barely five years after she pulled up stakes their daddy, Frank Logan, rode off one morning and never came back. For a while it was thought that Frank might have met with foul play, but if he had, his body was never found. After a time folks just figured he had gotten a bellyful of trying to raise those five boys.

Padgett also thought it was Pots and Leonard that Luke was looking for because they were the only two Logan boys who had not been seen around town for a couple of months. Then just three or four days earlier they had shown up with their pockets apparently full of money; they had been buying rounds of drinks every night in the Sagebrush Saloon.

Sheriff Padgett also said there was an uncle by the name of Raymond Logan who lived in Lubbock and had two boys of his own. They were both of about the same stamp as these five. R. W., the oldest, had been in trouble any number of times for stealing and robbery, and had almost been sent to prison a few years back for ambushing a traveling brush salesman who had been shot five times and robbed. Hard as Padgett tried, he had never been able to prove it even though he knew in his own heart that R. W. had done the shooting. The killing remained unsolved.

R. W.'s brother was twice as bad. Toby was the younger of the two, meaner than all get out, faster than a rattlesnake with his six-gun, and always hankering to use it. Because all seven boys were so close Padgett figured Lubbock to be Pots' destination when he had ridden north late in the evening two days earlier.

Leonard was a different deal. The sheriff had seen him just that morning coming out of the cafe across the street. Luke thanked the sheriff for his help and walked out of his office.

After taking a quick look around town and not finding the men or anyone who had seen them, Luke saddled up and rode south to the Logan farm. He arrived to find no one, but the door of the shack was standing open and inside the house the stove was still warm.

Luke found horses in the corral standing at the manger filled with fresh hay. He called out to let anyone who could hear know he was there, but got no reply. His eyes slowly scanned the brush at the back of the shack, but the search revealed nothing. Even though he had not seen or heard anyone, Luke had the feeling that someone was there. Whoever it was did not want to be found and was probably hunkered down nearby watching Luke's every move.

A short time later, Luke rode back to town stopping first at the livery where he put Mousy in a stall. After toting water to fill the trough, he gave him some grain. Luke then made his way along the boardwalk to the last place the sheriff had seen Leonard Logan. As he entered the cafe the smell of food cooking caused hunger pains to stir in his belly, and before long Luke was seated at a little table having a fine bowl of stew and a big slab of cornbread. More importantly, he was washing it all down with something more pleasing than a breath of fresh morning air—a good hot cup of strong coffee.

As Luke ate, he let his mind drift back over what Sheriff Padgett had said about the five Logan boys. All had been in trouble any number of times for robbery and stealing, but despite all that Padgett knew the Logans had done they all remained free because he could never find anyone willing to testify against one while the other four were still running loose.

"I don't have a fight with no one but Pots and Leonard," Luke said to himself in a tired, low voice. Then he thought, . . . *that is unless the others want to deal themselves a hand. And if they do, well, that's up to them. But if I can, I'm taking Pots and Leonard back to Rising Star to stand trial for murder. And I don't really care whether or not the brothers or their cousins like it.*

By the time Luke had finished his meal and walked back out onto the boardwalk it was nearly dark. The sun had dropped below the horizon and in many of the windows along the street the flicker of lanterns could be seen.

On the far end of town two old men made their way along the busy boardwalk, one carrying a ladder, the other, a rod with a flame on the end. When they came to a pole where a lantern hung, one would steady the ladder while the other climbed up and lit the light. And as each wick came to life the street emerged in the glow of lamp light.

The sound of a piano caught Luke's attention, and he looked across the way where the toe-tapping sound came from a brightly-lit saloon; but it was not the Sagebrush the sheriff had mentioned. A newly painted sign on the window read Trail's End.

Luke let his eyes drift slowly along the wide, dirt street to the far end where in the dim light he spotted what he was looking for—a big white sign with black letters that read Sagebrush Saloon. He hitched his pants and started toward it with the idea of finding the killers or someone who might know where to find them. His hopes faded as he entered and saw only two men inside.

One was the bartender, a short, stocky man with thinning hair and a full beard of a light red color. He stood behind the bar wiping its top with a rag but looked up, gave a welcoming smile, and spoke aloud, "Evenin' friend," as Luke walked in.

The other man sat in a dimly-lit corner at the rear of

the saloon near the back door and did not look up when Luke entered. He sat with his head tilted so that his hat blocked his face from view. A nearly empty whisky bottle and a newly filled glass were in front of him on the table.

As Luke walked into the long, narrow room the bartender asked, "What'll it be friend?"

"Give me a beer," Luke answered. Then propping an elbow on the bar, he said, "I'm looking for the Logan boys, Pots and Leonard. You seen 'em?"

The bartender's face turned white at the question. Then noticing the badge pinned to Luke's shirt his eyes instantly shifted to the man sitting in the corner. With an easy nod in that direction he said in a whisper, "Sid and Billy were in earlier but they drug out better than an hour ago. I ain't seen Pots or Kirk in a couple of days, but if 'n you're looking for Leonard, that's him sittin' there."

Luke glanced up at the mirror above the bar and saw the man's reflection. He was a shabby-looking man of average build, with long, black hair and clothes that were old and worn. He sat staring into his glass of whisky completely unaware of the conversation between Luke and the bartender.

Slowly, Luke reached down to slip the leather thong from the hammer of his Colt. When he turned from the bar his feet were spread wide and his right hand positioned just above the butt of his six-gun. His voice was loud and clear. "Leonard Logan . . . my name is Luke Ludd. I'm the sheriff of Rising Star and I'm here to take you back to stand trial for the murders of two friends of mind, Tom and Beth Tidwell. I believe you and your brother Pots killed 'em a few weeks back down in Rising Star."

The man looked up from his drink then, sliding his chair back slowly, pushed up to his feet and said in a deep, growling voice. "You must not know who I am, Mister. I'm Leonard Logan, and nobody named Logan gets arrested anywhere, whether it's here, in Rising Star, or anyplace else for that matter. So if I was you, I'd turn around and leave while you can still walk, because unless you're faster with your gun than me, I don't reckon you'll be arresting nobody for nothin'. And if you did happen to get the job done, which I seriously doubt you can— but say you did get it done—my brothers would have you dead before you get me halfway across the street."

"If I was you," Luke said calmly, "the first thing I'd do is shut my mouth. It makes you sound stupid. Then I'd slowly take my gun out of its holster and put it there on the table and step away with my hands in the air. I don't want to kill you, Leonard, but I will and you can believe me when I say I won't lose any sleep over it."

"That's for sure what you're going to have to do, Sheriff. 'Cause I ain't figgerin' on givin' up my gun to you or nobody else. And from where I'm standing I don't see where you're going to be man enough to take it. Unless I've judged you wrong and you're faster with yours than I think you are."

"I don't want any shootin' in—," the bartender started, but before he could finish, Leonard Logan dropped his hand for his six-gun.

Luke's right hand flashed and the lead flew, striking Logan dead center in his left shirt pocket. Logan's face instantly went blank and his eyes opened wide. He staggered back on stiff legs, and his eyes locked on Luke's in a cold, lifeless stare. For an instant the outlaw was still standing, but he knew he was dead. He also knew he had been beaten badly on the draw, for his six-gun had not cleared leather. He desperately tried to speak, but made no sound. Confused, he stared blindly at his empty hand, then his knees buckled and he fell. His body was numb from the waist down, yet his mind was alive and clear. He tried again to speak and to see the face of the man who stood opposite him. He tried to frame a word but the notion faded. *This was how it felt to die.* His legs and hands thrashed for an instant as if he was trying to stand, then the last rush of air came from his lips and when it was gone so was the life of Leonard Logan.

"By golly you killed 'im!" the bartender called out while making his way from behind the bar. "You killed Leonard Logan . . . you sure did, Mister. You beat 'im fair and square . . . I saw it. And look there," he said pointing. "His gun is still in the holster."

Luke turned back to the bar without reply, then picking up his beer, he turned it up. When he put it down again it was empty.

Only moments had passed when the bat-wing doors pushed open, and Luke saw Sheriff Padgett walk in from behind him came the sound of loud voices as a crowd quickly gathered in the street.

The sheriff slowly walked over to examine the body, then turned to call out for a couple of men to come take the dead man to the undertaker. Turning back to Luke he said, "You've killed a Logan and when the others hear 'bout it they'll all be coming after you. You better watch your step, Luke. One at a time a man can handle, but all of 'em together will be like a pack of wolves on a newborn calf."

Luke gave an understanding nod and answered, "I hope they don't, Sheriff, but if that's what they've got in mind there's really nothing I can do to stop 'em, I'll just have to deal with 'em if and when it happens." After taking a moment to think, Luke said, "Anyway, Sheriff, if we're finished here I think I'll mosey on down to the hotel and see if I can get some rest. I've got a long ride ahead of me startin' at first light."

Padgett shook his head, "No need in that. You can bunk down in one of the cells over in the jail if you want to. They're all empty and it won't cost you anything. The bed won't be as soft, I can tell you that much, but it'll be a bed nonetheless."

Luke gave a thankful nod, "Much obliged, Sheriff. Sound's good to me." Turning, he made his way out the door and across the street to the jail where he found an empty bunk and lay down. But like the other times he'd been forced to take a life, sleep did not come easily. Every time he closed his eyes he saw Leonard Logan's face and his cold, dead stare.

When Luke did finally doze off, it was only for a few minutes before his eyes opened again and he lay awake staring at the ceiling. The restless night's sleep made for an early rise, and well before sunup Luke and Padgett had coffee at the café.

At the livery, Luke threw the saddle on Mousy and after pulling the cinch tight he swung up to leather and rode north from Sweetwater in the direction of Lubbock where he figured he would have to kill Pots Logan.

Shortly before midday, Luke had found where Pots had left the main trail and taken to the brush. Off the trail Pots was no better at covering his tracks and Luke did not understand why he had gone to the trouble; if Pots had stayed on the main trail the travel would have been easy and fast. But he had taken to the brush and that was the trail Luke would follow.

For the next two days, Luke rode day and night stopping only to let Mousy rest and build a little fire to cook a quick cup of coffee. For the past three days the trail had been so fresh Luke had not taken a chance on building a fire for fear Pots might spot it.

Now Luke lay perfectly still, looking through a clump of grass at the last of the two men who he was sure had killed the Tidwells. He knew he was just one shot away from marking the debt owed those two fine people *Paid in Full.*

Luke glanced back at the fire to see Pots had poured another cup and as he took it up to his mouth he said, "You just going to shoot me outright, or are you goin' to give me a fightin' chance?"

Since Pots knew he was there, Luke answered, "I'll give you more of a chance than y'all gave those two old folks in Rising Star, but no more than I gave that murdering brother of yours back in Sweetwater."

"That old man kept hollerin' and carrying on . . . he

should have just gave us the money. That's all we wanted." There was a long pause, and with the cup still to his mouth, Pots asked, "You killed Leonard, did you?"

"Yes, sir," Luke answered, "sure did. He's visiting with the devil right now."

Pots forced a chuckle, "He sure might be. And if 'n he is you can bet he's givin' that old rascal trouble." Then he asked, "Were you alone when you killed 'im?"

"Yes, sir, I was."

"You must be a purty fair hand with your six-gun, Mister, 'cause Leonard was mighty fast with his, and a dead shot."

"I don't know for sure, but maybe he was just a dead shot when it came to killin' old, defenseless women and men. To be honest, Pots, I really don't know what kind of shot he was for sure, 'cause his gun never cleared leather. Matter a fact, his hand never made it as far as touching the butt."

"You don't say," Pots mumbled. "Was any of my brothers with 'im?"

"No, just him. But I did give him the same two choices that I'll give you, Pots. Either put your hands up or die. He chose the latter. I reckon he figured it was better than hangin' and that's for sure what would have happened if I'd taken 'im back. Somethin' for you to think 'bout too, Pots. You're going to hang if I take you back. We can take care of it now if you want to, or back in Rising Star, it's up to you, but either way I'm a-thinking you're a dead man."

"A dead man," Pots echoed. "Oh, I don't know so much 'bout that. Hell, you ain't beat me yet."

"You're right, I haven't. But I will and I think you know it."

Pots gave his head an easy nod and said, "We'll know more 'bout that here in a bit, but first I want to say that I am obliged for the thoughtfulness." He slowly took a sip and without taking the cup from his mouth, he dropped his right hand for his six-gun.

There was a loud roar and instantly the bottom of the tin cup exploded. The impact of the bullet drove Pots' head back with so much force his old black hat flew high in the air, catching on a limb in a nearby tree. He flipped over backwards and landed flat on his back on the ground. But he was unaware because he was already dead.

Luke did not move until well after the smoke had cleared, then he pushed slowly to his feet and made his way to where the outlaw lay dead. It was then that he looked down and said in a low, uncaring voice, "I'm not one to say, Pots, but I sure think you and Leonard both made the right choice."

Luke went to where he had tied up Mousy and after leading him back to camp, he stripped the saddle. Taking up a handful of dry grass he rubbed him down. He led Mousy to a small clearing just a little way from camp where Logan's horse was hobbled in a stand of cottonwoods. He put hobbles on Mousy and the horse instantly dropped his head to nibble at the tall, tender grass.

Back at camp, Luke added wood to the fire, and coffee to the pot. He sliced bacon into a skillet and while it cooked, he wrapped Logan's body in the bedroll that had been rolled out but never used. When Luke was finished, he started back toward the fire lost in thought. *At first light, I'll load the body over the saddle and head back to Sweetwater and drop off Pots so he can be buried alongside his brother. From there I'll ride home to Rising Star, back to Loraine and Jack Elam.*

The thought of his wife and son brought a smile to his unshaven face, then a long, lonely sigh from his lips, for he had not seen them since finding the Tidwells dead and riding from Rising Star more than three weeks earlier. Now with the Logan brothers dead, Luke's job was done and he could head back in the right direction.

When his food was ready, Luke squatted on his heels and poured a hot cup of coffee—his first in three days. The dry spell was not because he did not have any coffee—the truth was he had an almost full pound bag of good Arbuckle in his saddlebag. But with the trail fresh Luke had known he was getting closer to the man he sought, and did not want to take a chance on building a campfire and having the outlaw spot it.

After giving the hot coffee a quick cooling blow he took a sip and as expected found it mighty tasty, so tasty in fact that he drank the cup dry and filled it again before he began to eat. As he chewed, his thoughts were filled again with the two people who meant more to him than life itself, his beautiful wife Loraine, and son Jack Elam.

He smiled as he remembered the night Jack Elam was born and the hard time Loraine had had naming the little fellow. She had wanted to name him "Luke" after his daddy which made Luke proud, but seeing no need for two Lukes in one family, he had mentioned that it might be nice to name the baby after his grandfathers.

The next day, Loraine came up with the name, Luther Jack Elam Ludd. Luther, after Luke's father, and Jack, after her father, Cork; Elam was her uncle's name.

When Luke asked why she had chosen three names instead of just two like most folks, Loraine smiled and answered, "Well, Luke, you know Uncle Elam and how easy he gets his feelings hurt. I'm afraid that if I don't include him in naming our first baby he would never forgive me." Then she caught Luke by surprise, telling him his father-in-law's given name was not Cork, but Randall Jack Langtry. Cork was a name his daddy had given him when he was a baby.

With the bacon eaten and the last of the coffee drunk, Luke shook out his bedroll and crawled in, but tired as he was sleep did not come easily. Each time he closed his eyes the image of Tom and Beth Tidwell lying dead appeared.

"Why did this happen?" he asked himself in a low voice. They were fine people. Just two old folks who never did harm to anyone, who would go out of their way to do whatever they could to help a person, any person, whether someone they knew or a total stranger.

They had no money to speak of, only what little they had made selling their vegetables and Luke knew, as did everyone else in Rising Star, that a good portion was given away to folks who could not pay. They had spent their lives trying to help others. Now, for no good reason, they were dead, shot to death by two so-called men who had probably never done an honest day's work in their lives.

At one time this hard land was ruled by such men— men who wandered from one place to the next, murdering, stealing and raping, and when there was nothing left, moving on, leaving behind death and destruction.

Beaten down, the people cried out for law and order, and since then the number of outlaws had steadily decreased. Many had ended their lawless lives at the end of a rope while others had suddenly gone into other lines of work. But Luke knew there were still far too many who were more than willing to continue the sorry tradition of getting something for nothing.

"Why am I doing it?" Luke mumbled to himself, but immediately remembered Loraine and Jack Elam. And as he pulled down his hat to shield his eyes from the bright glow of the fire he said aloud, "That's two good reasons right there—and the only two I need."

At first light, Luke saddled the horses. He started a pot of coffee and, while it warmed, tried to throw Pots Logan's body over the saddle. But as he approached, the horse's ears shot forward and his nostrils flared at the sight of the unfamiliar shape of the bedroll. Smelling death, the horse let out a loud blow and shied away.

Luke tried a second time but got the same results. He then tied the horse between two trees where it stood nervously but let Luke load the body and secure it, tying hands to feet.

Back at the fire he poured a cup of coffee and took a sip. The hot liquid seemed to force blood through his body, suddenly bringing him to life. He thought of the long ride home, but also of how happy he would be to see Loraine and Jack Elam.

"Oh, how I miss those two," he mumbled. He always missed them when he was away, but he could not remember ever missing them quite this badly. They always seemed to be on his mind. This was a bad thing and Luke knew it. A man doing his job did not need anything but what he was doing on his mind—especially if he was tracking someone who would kill him given the chance. Something suddenly entered his mind for the first time. Was being sheriff of Rising Star the job he really wanted?

Luke had the ranch his paw had worked many years to have and in the end had given his life to keep. There was more than enough land and cattle to make a nice living and Luke knew it. But it was not money that drove him. It was something else—something deep inside him that had led him into his line of work. Although he could not put his finger on exactly what it was, it had been there since he was barely old enough to walk.

Luke stood, flipping the last few drops of coffee from his cup. He kicked dirt on the fire snuffing the flames to a few scattered wisps of white-gray smoke. He slowly made his way to where Mousy was tied and after packing the coffee pot and cup in his saddlebag, he gathered the reins and the other horse's lead rope and climbed into the saddle.

The sun was peeking over the eastern horizon, and soon its rays would lay hot upon the land. Big, white, puffy clouds dotted the pale-blue morning sky and beneath them a red-tailed hawk squawked while riding a current of wind.

After settling into the saddle, Luke touched Mousy with a spur and the horse moved out. Instead of riding south along the trail he had travelled to get there, Luke swung east to ride until he met the main trail leading south to Sweetwater, knowing it would be easier and faster.

He had not ridden far when he suddenly remembered what Sheriff Padgett had said about the three remaining Logan brothers coming after him when they learned he had killed Leonard. If they were coming, the main trail was the last place Luke wanted to be since it would put him right out in the open with no cover much of the time. If indeed the Logans had learned of the death of their brother, and by now Luke was sure they had, they probably also knew that Luke had left Sweetwater trailing Pots. It only made sense to assume they would know where he had gone after leaving town. If Padgett was right and the Logans were coming, Luke knew they could be anywhere. His eyes slowly scanned the countryside around him but saw nothing. Still, giving in to his better judgment, he decided it would be better to stay in the brush and swung Mousy back south.

Chapter Two

Tired and hungry and two days south of where the shoot-out with Pots Logan had taken place, Luke had made camp well before sundown in a stand of cottonwood that grew tall and green from the rocky bank of a dry creek bed. From under one of those large rocks a spring seeped up from deep within the earth and trickled down the bank into a narrow, man-made hollow to form a little pool. There were tracks—none fresh—but they all had been left by moccasins or bare feet, leading Luke to the conclusion that the hollow had been made several days ago, and by Indians. He also knew that in this hot, dry country where water was scarce, if one Indian knew about the spring, they all did, or would soon.

To the east no more than twenty yards away the brush opened to a clearing about one hundred yards deep and half that distance across. It was edged on three sides by mesquite and scrub cedar thick and tangled. From one side to the other the little clearing was covered ankle deep with rich green bunch grass.

Since making camp, Luke had taken some much-needed time from the saddle, and from the spring had drunk his fill of the cool, sweet water, and filled his canteens. With the light of day gone, he now sat in the glow of a small campfire watching bacon fry while sipping a freshly-boiled cup of coffee.

If things went well, he would be in Sweetwater the day after tomorrow. After reporting to Sheriff Padgett, he would drop off the body at the undertaker's and head to Rising Star.

He had seen nothing of the Logan bunch or for that matter anyone else. But the previous day he had come upon a trail that ran parallel to the one he was traveling. It was not finding the trail that bothered him for he knew that people came and went everyday across this land and when they did they naturally left a trail. It was what the trail showed that bothered him. There were six sets of tracks. Five horses definitely had riders and rode alongside the trail, two on one side and three on the other. The sixth horse was pulling a travois down the middle. That horse too, might also have been carrying a rider but with the travois dragging heavily on the ground it distorted the tracks leaving Luke unable to tell for sure.

What got his attention was that the tracks were heading south, the same direction Luke was traveling, and none of the animals were shod, a sure sign of Indians, five, possibly six. Because the Indian's main use for a travois was to haul what few belongings they had, or to carry the sick or elderly, Luke figured it was a small group, probably a family moving from one place to another.

Still they were Indians, and knowing their hostility toward white men, Luke would be doing himself a great injustice to take their presence lightly. And if the Indians were not enough to keep him on his toes there were still the Logan boys. Were they hiding along the trail waiting for Luke to ride within their sights to have their revenge? Or would they come in darkness while Luke was asleep, to storm his camp with guns blazing? Or had Padgett figured wrong and the Logan boys would not come at all? Only time would tell.

The Logans were bound to know their brothers had killed the Tidwells; surely Pots or Leonard had said something to one of them. If not, where did they think those two had gotten the money to buy drinks? Luke was almost positive the brothers had to know. They also had to know the law would not let Leonard and Pots kill two innocent people without paying for their crime. From all accounts the Logans were a tightly-knit bunch, and perhaps did not figure killing was a crime. They might have figured killing to be part of living and something that was done to get by.

After throwing more wood on the fire, Luke took the rope from his saddle and tied a line between two trees. He made his way to the clearing where the horses were hobbled, led them back to camp, and tied them off, each on one side of the line facing opposite directions. If someone should try to approach the camp—white man or Indian—the horses would sense their presence and alert him well in advance of danger.

Luke shook out his bedroll and spread it on the ground near the fire. He carefully placed Pots Logan's body down and covered him with a blanket. Then he placed Pots' old hat over his face as if it were shielding his eyes from the glare of the fire.

Luke wanted it to appear to anyone watching or approaching that he was asleep in his bedroll. When he was satisfied with the camp he picked up his extra blanket and Winchester, and walked away from his camp in the direction of a towering cottonwood he had scouted earlier. It was about ten yards east of camp, in the shadows and out of reach of the glow of the flickering campfire.

A few feet beyond the tree a thick entanglement of thorny briers three feet high formed a nearly impassable barrier fifty feet long, with the old cottonwood smack in the middle. Near the tree trunk, Luke dropped cross-legged to the ground and after draping the blanket around his shoulders, laid the rifle across his lap.

From his position he had a clear view in all directions except behind him, but with the wall of briers behind him he did not have to worry about anyone sneaking into camp from that direction.

In the eastern sky only a half moon hung high among the thin, wispy clouds. Where its soft glow could penetrate the thick canopy of branches and leaves moonlight dotted the ground. A slight breeze blew warm out of the south, from time to time gusting and stirring the leaves in the trees.

From a branch high above an owl hooted. A moment later and to the north, a nightingale called to his mate. Then from the not-too-distant west a coyote cried his loneliness to the moon and was almost instantly answered.

These were familiar sounds that Luke expected to hear, sounds that belonged to the prairie and the night. He listened more closely for the misplaced sounds that would tell him danger was near. It would be reacting in the right manner to those sounds that would hopefully keep him alive.

Luke leaned back against the trunk of the massive old cottonwood and for a brief moment closed his eyes. That was just enough time for his mind to fill with thoughts of Loraine and Jack Elam, Rising Star, and home.

The images of the little white house seemed to linger as he recalled the last time he had seen it. Loraine had been standing on the front porch holding Jack Elam in her arms and waving as he rode off. That was the day he discovered the Tidwells. Before taking to the killers' trail, he had gone home to tell Loraine what had happened and to pick up a few supplies.

Loraine did not ask him in so many words, but Luke knew by the way she nervously held his hand, and the look of worry and doubt in her beautiful brown eyes that she did not want him to go. That much was obvious. But it was his job to defend the people who had been wronged and could no longer defend themselves. It was his sworn duty to go after the man or men responsible for this unthinkable crime and bring them to justice no matter what it took. Luke knew Loraine understood, but he also knew she did not want him to go.

Then as if it were only yesterday, Luke thought back to their wedding day and how happy he was to be marrying such a beautiful and loving woman. The next day they had moved into the stone house on Luke's family place, and just a little over a year later Jack Elam was born.

The year after the baby came along the folks of Rising Star voted Luke their sheriff. It was a job he had not campaigned for and a job he had not really wanted or needed since he had more than enough to do just looking after the ranch. But after weeks of pleading from the townfolk, Luke took the job with the understanding that he would need a deputy, and the town would have to build a house for him since he had a family. The backroom of a jail was no place to raise a baby.

The town leaders happily agreed. Tall, red-headed Slim Fathree became the new deputy and a little white house at the edge of town was built. As it happened, the house was built on the very spot Luke had shot and killed Maxwell Laughlin, the man who had ordered Luke's daddy killed.

Since moving into town Loraine had been much better about Luke's being gone. Mrs. Bitters, an old family friend whom Loraine looked to as a mother—and who had helped Doc McFarland bring Jack Elam into the world—was always stopping by to check on her and the baby and taking them cake or cookies. Otherwise Loraine and the baby were over at Mrs. Bitters' doing something.

The company kept Loraine from being lonely when Luke was away but did little to keep her from missing the ranch life. And it didn't do much at all to ease the loneliness she felt not having her paw and Uncle Elam around. It had been only six months since the move to town, and Luke hoped as time went on that Loraine would adjust. If not there would be nothing to do but load up and move back home. Luke would never ask his wife to stay where she did not want to be.

Loraine's daddy rode into town from time to time, but not often, and when Cork did, it was usually to sell some hogs or pick up a few supplies. On those trips he seldom had time to stay for a long visit. He would sometimes stay for supper, but never for the night. With two places to look after—his and Luke's—he was so busy he had hired a man to help out, a big, stout, hardworking drifter named Punkin Brown.

Elam had helped Cork for a while but for some reason, and without saying a word to anyone, had taken off for weeks or even months at a time. He had been spending a lot of time up on Beaver Mountain visiting Two Toes, the old Cheyenne Indian who had given them all a safe place to stay when the McKuens, on Maxwell Laughlin's orders, had put three bullets in Luke and left him for dead.

Thinking back to that dark night sent a cold chill through Luke's body as he remembered the pain of the bullets ripping his flesh. The first had hit him up high on the left shoulder, knocking him to the ground. The second cut deep and low into his left side; and the third almost took off his right leg below the knee.

Luke rubbed the numbness that lingered in his shoulder and at the indentation on the side of his leg where the bullet had entered. He recalled that Cork and Loraine had loaded him into the wagon and hauled him, unconscious for most of the way, to Beaver Mountain. On that mountain Luke had healed enough to again stand by himself. It was also where he, Elam, and Cork, along with Loraine and Two Toes, had held off another assault by the McKuens. And the next day they did it again when Roscoe Nash and his bunch of hired guns showed up.

"Things have really changed," he mumbled aloud. Then he thought: *If not for Pa getting killed I would never have come back. I'd still be a Pinkerton. I'd still be up north riding the rails, watching after the gold shipments.*

Suddenly the wind stirred and in the rustle of the leaves above he heard a child's voice say, "Daddy, I love you." As quickly as the tiny voice had come it was gone, leaving a man proud he was no longer a Pinkerton, and happy to be where he was rather than up north on a train.

Luke took a long, ragged breath and as he let it out, he looked slowly across the camp. When the horses came into view his eyes suddenly stopped. The bay stood quietly, but Mousy had seen or heard something and stood with his head high, ears perked, and nostrils flared.

As Luke straightened to take a better look he moved

his hand to the stock of his Winchester. In that instant the bay must have seen or heard movement because his head shot up. Something, or someone was out there. Luke's pulse quickened as he strained his eyes and ears to see and hear, but beyond the glow of the dying fire he saw nothing. The only sound was that of his own heart pounding.

Without moving his head, Luke slowly moved his eyes in the direction the horses were looking. It was not what he saw but what he heard that caught his attention. Beyond the dim glow of the campfire a muted chatter was coming from the creek bottom. There was a rustle of dry leaves and moments later a raccoon scampered from the darkness, suddenly stopping when it saw the horses. Then noticing the body of Pots Logan, the furry, masked creature perched on his hind legs and after a long moment of sniffing the air, turned and disappeared back into the brush. The chatter continued, but faded into the distance.

Once again dead quiet fell over the camp, and with the fire quickly dying, a terrible darkness.

If Luke wanted light, he would have to add wood to the fire and stoke it. But he knew any movement he made would give away his position to anyone watching. He had not heard or seen anything that led him to believe danger was near, but he had a feeling deep in his gut—a feeling that something was going to happen.

The south wind that had blown lightly earlier had picked up and with dampness the night had cooled considerably. The earlier gusts were now a steady wind that made the leaves hum and tall grass sway. Luke relaxed the Winchester back across his lap, then gathered the blanket and pulled it tight. Just as he started to lean back against the cottonwood he heard two loud swooshes followed by thuds as two arrows flew into Pots Logan's dead body.

The Indians screamed a loud death cry as they broke over the creek bank, but they had not taken many steps when Luke let fly a bullet in the direction of the first dark shadow. There was a low painful cry and the shadow nearest the fire instantly flipped over backwards to the ground near the fire.

Surprised by the unexpected gunshot, and not knowing where it had come from, the other shadow turned back toward the creek. As the figure broke over the rocky edge, Luke pulled another shot and the loud pop that followed told him it had struck flesh. The Indian tumbled head over heels disappearing into the creek bottom.

Luke quickly worked the lever on the Winchester again, but there were no more ear-piercing screams or shadows moving. He sat for a good half hour with his ear to the wind, his eyes searching the darkness. Then from the south the sound of horses at a gallop filled the cool night air, but moments later the hoof-beats faded into the night.

Still, Luke did not make any big moves or try to rise from his hiding place. Instead he hunkered more closely to the tree suspecting all the horses might not have ridden off. If it was the Indians from the trail he had found the day before, there could be as many as six. From the sound, even at a distance, he thought no more than three and possibly only two horses had galloped off.

Without moving his head, Luke slowly moved his eyes right, then left, but was not able to see more than arm's length in either direction and looked back at the camp. It was dark, though from time to time a flame leaped from the bed of hot coals. The flare-ups did not last long or produce enough light to see much of anything.

Luke could, however, make out the dark glob of a shadow where Pots Logan lay and another where the first Indian had fallen, and the horses still standing at the picket line.

Luke did not know the condition of the second Indian who had rolled down the bank. Was he dead? Or just wounded? If so, how badly was he hurt? He may have gotten back to his feet, made it to his horse and ridden off. Or he might have been merely nicked and was waiting for Luke to show himself so he could take a shot. Luke knew trying to find out now might be playing into his hands and decided to wait until first light when he could see to make a move.

What little fire that remained would soon be gone and in total darkness anyone moving would have to feel his way and a sound would be made—a hand into a thorny bush, or a foot coming down on a twig or dry leaves. Luke depended on hearing those sounds to tell him when danger was near.

On the other hand it could be over. Maybe the Indians had had enough. The horses were still at the picket line and Luke was sure they had been after the horses. The first attempt had left one Indian lying on the ground either dead or dying, and possibly another in the creek bottom. Luke knew Indians valued horse-flesh, but with two Indians already down they might figure the price for these horses was too high.

Another thought crossed his mind. Maybe the Indians had been after just a drink of water; but if water was all they wanted why had they come out of the creek bottom hollering and screaming? Why had they not just taken the water and left? The little pool in the creek bottom is completely out of sight and far enough away that they could have gotten all the water they had wanted, probably without Luke ever knowing. *No, it had to be the horses, or just their unwillingness to pass up the chance to kill a white man.*

The night had been long and restless, but darkness was giving way to the gray haze that came each morning just before sunup. It would not be long until Luke could see. He would then attempt to stand or move from behind his cover. Until then he would remain motionless, his eyes taking in all they could, and his ears straining to hear.

Suddenly, from the west a pack of coyotes cried in harmony to the fading moon. Moments later and no more than a hundred yards to the south a turkey gobbled a loud "Good morning," to his hens. In the eastern sky the first glimmer of sun was starting to peek over the tree-covered hills. With each passing moment the night was fading as light took its place.

Near the creek two armadillos eased along, each stopping from time to time to dig under a rock or through dry leaves in search of food. Luke knew with light quickly approaching, these armor-clad creatures were heading home and would soon be safe in their underground dens, not to reappear until darkness came again.

As Luke scanned the camp the shadow he had shot in the dark took shape. The Indian's shirtless, brown body lay sprawled where it had landed just a few feet from the fire. He wore pants made of buckskin, and a quiver of arrows was strapped over his back. He still clutched his bow in his left hand, and not far away a tomahawk lay harmless in the dust. Because of the dim morning light and the distance between Luke and the body, no other features could be distinguished.

Luke turned his attention to the horses that still stood quietly at the picket line, their eyes nervously following the armadillos as they slowly made their way along the creek bank. From the south the turkey gobbled again and the hens chirped back, and just moments later, a loud flutter of flapping wings echoed along the creek as the turkeys descended from their tree-top roost.

Satisfied that all was well, Luke took hold of a low-hanging limb and slowly pulled himself up straight. His joints were stiff, and his muscles sore from the long night of sitting. He propped his rifle against the tree, then stretched his arms high above his head and bent over touching the ground with his fingertips to ease the tightness from his weary body. Then he reached for his rifle and started from under the cottonwood.

Walking to where the Indian lay dead, Luke stopped to examine the body. His clothes and arm band were Comanche, but his beaded headband was definitely Kiowa. Flat on his back, his dark brown eyes were open wide to the hazy morning sky. A jagged hole marked where the bullet had entered his body in the center of his chest, and the small amount of blood surrounding the hole indicated he had died quickly.

Luke walked the few feet to where the other Indian had rolled down the bank. He noticed blood clinging to the grass and a bigger splatter covering the ground, but a quick study of the creek bottom revealed no body. Rifle at the ready, Luke started down the bank and when he reached the bottom he realized how badly the Indian had been hit. The leaves and grass where he had rolled to a stop were pushed flat. It was evident from the great amount of blood covering the leaves the injured man had lain there a good while bleeding profusely.

With the toe of his boot, Luke raked back some of the leaves to find the ground, too, was deeply and darkly soaked with blood. He stood up and looked south hoping to see the body, knowing no man with this kind of blood loss could go very far before collapsing; but there was nothing but empty creek bottom as far as his eyes could see.

"He couldn't have gone far," Luke mumbled under his breath. "He's lost too much blood." Then he thought, *He may still be alive. I don't see how, but he sure might be. If he is, I either need to help him or go ahead and finish the job. There's no need letting a person suffer—white man or Indian.*

And if he was shot down low in the gut, and could somehow get the blood stopped, Luke knew he might live for at least a couple of days before finally dying. "No, that wouldn't be right," he said aloud to himself. Then hitching his pants, he started following the blood trail, figuring he would not have to go far before finding the *body*.

Luke moved slowly and easily along the creek bottom with much caution, for he knew if the Indian had as much as a drop of blood left in him, he would still be dangerous. Three times, Luke found where the Indian had stumbled and fallen to the ground, but each time had somehow gotten back to his feet and moved on. In one spot he had reached a large cottonwood root along the bank, and had rested against the root.

Another fifty or sixty yards along the creek, Luke discovered a mingling of horse tracks, three sets in all. In addition to those there were three sets of tracks made by moccasins revealing that there had been three Indians in all. One left leaving the blood trail, another was back at camp dead, and the third had apparently waited with the horses to keep them quiet. At the mingled tracks the blood trail stopped.

Luke glanced at the cut on the west side of the creek bank where the three horses had made their way over the top. The Indians were gone for the moment but where and for how long Luke did not know. He figured at least one was watching from somewhere nearby and as soon as Luke broke camp and rode from view the Indians would come back. They might be content just to gather their dead and ride on, but they might come in greater numbers with the intention of trying to take the horses again. With the latter weighing heavily on his mind, he turned and headed back in the direction he had just come.

Back at camp, Luke stoked the fire then added wood, and as the flames grew, he placed the coffee pot where it would heat and saddled the horses.

After removing the two arrows from Pots Logan's decaying body, he loaded him over the saddle. He then made his way back to the fire where he squatted on his heels, and after pouring a cup of coffee gave it a cooling blow, and took a taste.

Luke glanced in the direction of the dead Indian and thought for a moment about burying him. But he knew there was really no need because once he rode off the others would come back for the body. Luke could not help wondering how such a great nation of people could end up as the Indians had. Their hunting grounds were steadily disappearing due to the invasion of the whites. Their buffalo were being killed and skinned by the thousands and their carcasses left lying on the prairie where they had fallen to rot in the hot sun.

The Indians themselves had been hunted and killed and their lands had been taken in the name of progress. Several times they had put their trust in what the white man had said. They had signed the white man's treaties time and again in hopes of making things better only to find that each time they had been cheated and deceived.

To Luke there was no mystery about why the Indians hated the white man as they did. He knew that if he had been treated the way whites had treated the Indians, he would hate the white man too.

With that awful thought in mind, Luke poured another cup and drank it slowly. When he had swallowed the last drop, he pushed to his feet and after giving his arms and back a good, long stretch, kicked dirt on the fire reducing the few remaining flames to light puffs of smoke. Crossing to where the horses were tied, he loaded the pot and cup into his saddlebag. Then stepping into leather, Luke bumped Mousy with a gentle spur and the horse moved out.

What little breeze did stir blew light from the south and at this early hour it lay damp and cool on Luke's face. But he knew as the sun rose higher in the pale-blue, cloudless sky the morning coolness would give way to the heat of the day. Turning in the saddle he glanced back at the horse carrying the body to see flies swarming thick around the bedroll where the blood from Pots Logan's wound had finally soaked through. "That's what I get for killing 'im," he mumbled to himself.

Suddenly from beside the bleached-out remains of a fallen cottonwood just a few feet off the trail there was slight movement followed by a loud flutter. Mousy instantly shied from the unexpected sound and his sudden sideways movement forced Luke to grab the pommel with one hand while dropping the lead rope and reaching down for his six-gun with the other. But realizing he had lost a stirrup and was slipping from the saddle, Luke gave up on drawing his pistol and grabbed at the pommel with both hands.

Luckily the unexpected commotion was not caused by ambushing Indians as Luke had so quickly imagined, nor was it the Logans. The near heart-stopping event was caused by nothing more than a turkey hen being flushed from her hiding place. With the saddle now back under him, Luke watched as the old gal glided to a landing along a distant line of brush.

Luke took the lead rope, but instead of holding it in his hand as he rode, he tied it in a slipknot and hung it over the pommel, leaving his right hand free.

Near midday, Luke spurred Mousy to the top of a high rocky ridge where there was an outcropping of six large, blackish-gray boulders that stood in a circle like mighty stone soldiers. In the center of that circle another massive boulder eaten away by wind and rain through the years had taken on the shape of what looked like a man carrying a washtub. The side facing west was straight and stretched up fifteen feet to an awkward-shaped top that resembled the head of a man wearing a flat-brimmed hat. Just under the brim on the east side were the face and neck. Below that, the rock broadened a span of more than four feet to form the chest before protruding about eight or ten feet to form the washtub. On the ground beneath that tub-shaped ledge was yet another circle of rocks and in that circle were the charred remains of a campfire.

Luke spun Mousy to have a look in all directions then turning back to face the overhang, said to himself in a low voice, "This will be a good spot."

He could let the horses rest here. And with hunger pains stabbing his insides this would be a good place to build a fire completely out of view of others.

After unloading the body and stripping the gear, Luke hobbled the horses on a small patch of grass a few yards downhill from camp. The grass grew in short, tight bunches, and there was not much of it, but it was grass and it was green. On his way back up the hill, Luke gathered kindling to start a fire, filled his coffee pot, also poured water from his canteen into a small pan, and placed both over the flames.

When the water started to boil, Luke added a couple pieces of jerked meat. While it cooked, he made his way to the northeast edge of camp and stood in the shadow of a stone soldier about five feet high and at least as wide. From there he had a clear view of his back trail and he was able to look carefully through the tree tops in that direction, but saw nothing unusual.

To the east a dust devil was building in the distance and beyond it another; they moved north simultane-ously blowing and twisting their way across the prairie. As the nearest one faded back into the earth, the other kept building, sending a giant plume of reddish-brown dust high into the air.

Luke turned his attention to the south, the direction

he would be riding when he left the camp and that the Logans would be coming from if they were coming after him. But he saw only a few scattered trees and beyond them miles of open prairie.

He had seen no evidence that the Indians who had attacked him were following, but he had noticed one thing that gave him reason for concern. Four or five miles back he had cut across a trail with the same markings he had come upon just two days earlier. The only difference was the trail he had crossed today was going from east to west, not north to south.

Luke had backtracked and found where the Indians had bedded down during the night, but nowhere had he found any sign of blood, and Luke knew if the Indian he had shot had gotten back to camp bleeding as he was, there would have been a sign of blood somewhere, even if he had been dead.

Luke also found that the Indians had ridden into their camp from a northerly direction, but there were no signs they had ridden back out again. The horse tracks showed the Indians had broken camp that morning and moved out toward the west. Apparently they had heard the gunfire during the night and decided to change direction. This Indian party had not attacked anyone—of that Luke was sure.

It could mean only one thing. The three Indians who had attacked were another band, and Luke had killed one, possibly two of them.

Again Luke moved his eyes along his back trail, but after a good bit of seeing only what God had put there, he made his way back to the overhang and the fire where his dinner was ready.

Later, with his belly full and the horses still needing rest, Luke walked back to the old stone soldier at the edge of camp and, in its shade, dropped cross-legged to the ground.

Looking north he again studied his trail with a slow careful eye, pausing from time to time to take a closer look at something that did not seem quite right, but in the end the intense search indicated nothing out of the ordinary. Still Luke had an awful feeling gnawing at his insides that sooner or later he would look and the Indians would be coming. He had killed one and shot another, and knew that as soon as the remaining Indians reached their camp—wherever that was—and told the others what had happened, they would be coming after him. Of that Luke had no doubt. The only thing Luke was not sure of at the present was when and where he would be when it happened.

Luke let his eyes drift south and, as he did, thought about riding on, for he knew Sweetwater could be no more than a day's ride. If he got caught out in the open, however, he would stand little chance. Here at least he had the advantage of food and cover, and he was up where he had a clear view in all directions. But his only water was what little was left in the canteens.

"No," Luke mumbled. Then he thought, *If it's going to happen, whether it's the Indians or the Logans, this will be a good place to make a stand.*

* * *

Hours later and for an unknown reason, Luke's eyes shot open to a day that was much farther along than he expected. The sun hung low in the western sky and the shadows around him stretched long and jagged to the east.

He slowly wiped the sleepy blur from his eyes with the back of his hand, and realizing he must have dozed off, hurriedly got to his feet and looked in the direction of the horses. They had been standing quietly with their heads down, nibbling at the grass, but both raised their heads and looked in his direction when he so abruptly stood up.

"This is a hell of a time to be trying to catch up on my shut-eye," Luke said, aggravated with himself, as he turned to have a look back along his trail. Finding all as before, he walked to the overhang to find the fire had died away, though the coffee pot was still warm to the touch. He added kindling to the fire, then dropping to one knee he blew at the smoldering ashes and the result was as expected. First came a light swirl of smoke, then another, then a small flicker of flame leaped up, and moments later the fire blazed back to life.

With the fire going and the coffee getting hot, Luke took up his Winchester and started back toward the boulder lookout, but had not taken many steps in that direction when a shadow passing along the ground caught his attention. He turned toward the heavens to see the light-blue, cloudless sky dotted thick with buzzards. Several more sat perched in the branches of a not-too-distant mesquite tree patiently waiting to move in.

Luke knew the buzzards had spotted Pots Logan's

dead body and would not be going anywhere until they had had their fill or the body was buried. He knew too, that the giant, black birds would not go unnoticed by the Indians or the Logans if they came his way. But the question had never been whether they would find him, but when and where.

Luke walked to the edge of camp, rested his left arm on the shoulder of the stone soldiers, and as he looked down at the trail the latter part of his question was answered. He saw dust—and a lot of it—rising above the tree tops to the distant north. "Here they come," he said aloud in a low, unsurprised voice.

Knowing there was not much time, he turned and made a dead run down the hill to where the horses grazed and after leading them back to camp, tied them in among the boulders. He took two boxes of cartridges from his saddlebag, and stacked both saddles in front of the overhang to give him some cover if the attackers stormed the camp and managed to somehow make their way past the stone guards.

Luke drew his colt and flipped open the cylinder, spun it slowly until satisfied it had a full load, shoved it back in place and latched it down. After making sure Pots Logan's pistol was also loaded, Luke stuck it deep into his waist band. He checked both Winchesters as well and started in the direction of the boulder at the edge of camp.

The cloud of dust had moved closer but was still better than a mile away and because of the density of the trees it was impossible to tell who or how many it was. It was not until they topped a rise and rode into a small clearing that Luke knew. It was Indians and from what he could tell there were about a dozen.

The Indian riding in front suddenly reined in his horse and cast his eyes toward the sky. Luke knew they had spotted the buzzards and it would be just a matter of time before they came to investigate. He also knew that if they all came at once he would need to do away with at least four on their first charge if he was going to have any chance of getting out alive. His thoughts turned to Loraine and Jack Elam and for a brief moment he wondered if he would ever see them again, but those terrible thoughts were cut short when the Indians began to advance.

They rode slowly through the brush for another hundred and fifty yards before the leader raised his hand and stopped in a little stand of trees. He spun his horse and said something to the others, and when they started again, three broke away riding west and three more swung east, leaving the leader and three more coming from the north.

"They're splitting up," Luke mumbled to himself. At least he knew now there was a total of ten Indians, not twelve as he had first thought. Even with them split up, Luke knew ten was still a good number to try to keep an eye on. At least he had not seen any signs of rifles or pistols, which led him to believe his soon-to-be attackers were armed only with bows, arrows, and lances.

Luke considered his situation as he watched the Indians ride. The three circling east were the least of his worries because, to get anywhere near him, they would either have to ride all the way around and come in from due south along the line of thick brush, or they could take a chance and try to cross the little clearing just to the east, but he figured they would be too smart to make a mistake like that.

He was going to have to watch closest the three riding west because they could ride to within seventy-five yards before having to leave the cover of brush. In those seventy-five yards the earth dipped to form a little valley. Luke knew a man on horseback could still be seen in the bottom of that swag, but a man on foot, or crawling, would be out of sight until he stuck up his head on the near side. It was seeing those three Indians move into the swag and figuring out where they would show themselves that would determine whether Luke would get off a clean, fast shot or they would get to him.

Luke looked back north to see two of the four Indians had dismounted; the other two sat astride their ponies watching the buzzards circling overhead.

Luke also turned his eyes toward the sky, where it was not the buzzards that caught his attention, but the position of the sun. It hung very low in the western sky with only a very thin line of blue between its golden rays and the darkness of the distant horizon. It would be dark soon and he knew if the Indians did not make a move until the sun fell below the horizon the advantage would be theirs.

"Maybe they'll wait until morning," Luke mumbled to himself, and the thought was still bouncing around in his mind when the two Indians on the ground suddenly stood.

"I see you've got yourself in quite a pickle," a voice from behind said.

Luke spun at the unexpected voice with his rifle raised.

"Hold up there, Luke," the voice said. "It's me, Elam."

"Elam," Luke echoed with a smile. "Where in the world did you come from?"

"Oh, just out lookin' at the country and seen this hill here. Thought I'd mosey over this way and see if I could find somebody maybe needin' a little help." Then with a short chuckle Elam asked, "You need some help, do you?"

Luke gave a playful nod. "Yes, sir, looks like I might be needin' a hand if you ain't got something else to do."

Elam pointed west with his rifle barrel. "There's three working around, I reckon they're going to try to cross that swag."

Luke jerked his head to the north. "There's four right down there and three more making their way east."

"Seen 'em," Elam said, "And one of 'em is wearing a union coat." Then, noticing the blood-soaked bedroll he asked, "Who we got over there? Pots Logan?"

Luke gave a nod, "Yes, sir, that's who it is alright. Him and his brother killed the Tidwells. How did you know?"

Elam sadly shook his head, "Yeah, that's bad, I talked to Cork when I got back from Beaver Mountain and he told me about what happened. I don't know why anybody would want to hurt those two old folks. Those two old people never did anybody any harm."

"I took care of his brother back in Sweetwater."

"That's how I found you. And that's how I knew that

was Pots Logan in that bedroll," Elam replied. "I talked to the sheriff, and he told me about the gunfight and that you were headed this way. From what he said you might have more than just a few Indians on your trail . . . you might have the rest of those Logan boys coming after you, too."

"There's three more of 'em," Luke started, but his words were cut short when the four Indians to the north began to move. "Here they come."

.

Chapter Three

Elam pointed north. "Those four there are just decoys. The ones we need to be concerned with are these over here on the west side. I'll go see if I can keep an eye on 'em and you watch those there."

Luke gave an understanding nod and, after watching Elam go, turned back to watch the four Indians coming from the north. But a slight movement caught his eye and he looked east to see that the three Indians he figured would ride around and try to come up from the south had circled back and were approaching the clearing. At that moment the quiet of the late evening was shattered by the deafening report of a rifle, and then another.

Instantly the Indians both to the north and at the clearing let out loud, ear-piercing war cries and kicked their ponies into full run. Since the Indians at the clearing were closest Luke threw up his rifle in that direction and pulled off a quick shot.

The Indian leading the way grabbed his chest with both hands and began to sway atop his horse. For an instant he grabbed at the horse's mane trying to stay on but with life slipping away he tumbled backwards and hit the ground in a hard, sliding bounce.

Luke quickly worked the action on his Winchester and pulled off a second shot just as the Indian's horse side-stepped a sagebrush and the bullet missed its target by a good bit. It kicked up some dust well behind the charging Indian when it harmlessly struck the ground. Luke worked the lever again but before he could get off another shot an arrow struck the boulder just inches from his head and when it ricocheted, the shaft struck Luke squarely in the left eye.

Luke threw up a defending hand and blinked at the stinging pain that instantly filled his eye, at the same time mopped at the water that suddenly ran down his cheek with the back of his hand. He desperately wiped and blinked trying to clear the watery blur that quickly spread to both eyes.

Hearing footsteps behind him, Luke spun to see a blurred buckskin-dressed outline coming from behind a boulder. Knowing Elam was dressed in buckskin, Luke hesitated, but when the blurred shape let out a shrilling scream Luke instinctively jerked up his rifle and pulled the trigger. At the same moment a rifle roared from the west. Two loud thuds simultaneously echoed among the boulders when the bullets had struck flesh and the Indian let out a low muffled groan and tumbled head-over-heels, stopping only a foot from where Luke stood. The Indian, with tomahawk in hand, clawed and kicked at the rocky ground trying to advance but his strength was quickly fading. Finally he relaxed his head to the earth and when a last final gasp for life failed, all movement stopped and the Indian lay dead.

Luke spun back at the sound of horse hooves to see the Indian he had shot and missed riding straight for him. Luke sidestepped the charging horse but as he did the Indian leaped and Luke, still clutching his rifle, threw up his left hand to stop the downward plunge of the Indian's knife, and with his right, blocked the swing of the tomahawk. When their bodies slammed together the force was so great it knocked the rifle from Luke's hand, at the same time driving him back hard against the boulder, the sudden impact forcing the air from his lungs.

Luke gasped for air but at the same instant knew he could not wait for it. For a brief moment Luke glanced past the Indian in front of him at yet another blurry outline coming up the hill, on a horse also at a full run, but just as that Indian started to leap, the rifle from the west roared and the Indian slumped, grabbing for the horse's neck. As the horse turned away from the dusty commotion the rider lost his grip and fell dead to the ground.

Locked in hand-to-hand combat the Indian tried to push the blade of his knife into Luke's flesh but when the attempt failed he tried to swing his tomahawk. In that split second, Luke sidestepped and spun the Indian against the boulder, then came up hard with a knee right into the Indian's belly, at the same time banging the hand holding the tomahawk hard against the rock until the tomahawk came loose. Luke suddenly released his grip and came across with a hard right, catching the Indian squarely in the mouth and, in the same motion, dropping his hand for his six-gun.

The Indian lunged forward but just as he did Luke pulled the trigger. The flame and lead flew from the barrel of the pistol causing a short-lived flare around the center button of the old union coat. The Indian's body stiffened, his dark brown eyes widened, and his face twisted with pain. He staggered back but the boulder stopped him and he stood on stiff legs, his eyes locked on Luke's. His mouth moved as though he was trying to speak but only bright, red blood gushed out. His body began to tremble, his knees buckled, and he slowly slid down the face of the dark gray boulder to the ground where, like many before him, his lifelong fight with the white man slowly came to an end.

Luke holstered his pistol, made his way to where he had dropped his rifle, picked it up and, after feeding a bullet into the chamber, moved behind one of the stone soldiers and dropped to one knee. Elam's rifle roared again. Luke tried wiping the fluid running from his left eye to clear his vision but stopped when he realized his eye was too painful to blink or be touched with any pressure.

Suddenly a loud, shrill cry from the north brought Luke to his feet. He looked in that direction to see the Indian who had led the raiding party sitting on his horse out of rifle range. The late evening air came alive with the sound of horses at a gallop as three others rode in from different directions to join him.

For a good while they just sat looking at the hill and from time to time one would spin his horse and let out a loud whoop and holler. One started a charge but had not gone far before the leader called him back. They sat and watched for a bit longer. Then, as slowly as they had come, they turned their ponies and rode off to the north.

"I'm gettin' too darn old for this," Elam said.

Luke turned too see Elam coming along the trail. "I'm glad you showed up when you did. They would have had me for sure."

"Oh, I don't know about that," Elam said as he walked up to Luke. "If I hadn't come along you would have been over on the west side behind those bigger boulders yonder, and those two couldn't have just rode in on you the way they did. I left two of 'em lying at the edge of that swag dead, and wounded another. Looked to me like I hit 'im down low on the side of the neck—can't say how bad he's hit though. All I know for sure is he let out one heck of a scream and as he went down he grabbed his neck."

"There's two more here, and another lying out there in the clearing," Luke cut in. "That's five dead for sure and one with a neck wound, and four rode off. That accounts for all ten."

Elam motioned with a hand, "Anyway, let's go over by the fire so I can have a look at that eye, looks to me like you came close to losing it."

"Don't think it would have hurt any worse if I had."

At the fire Elam took the bandana from around his own neck and after folding it, he soaked it with hot coffee from the pot. "Here, take this and after it cools a little put it over your eye. It's going to hurt like hell, Luke, but the heat will ease the pain and slow down the swelling a mite."

Hesitantly, Luke took the hot poultice and after giving it some thought he very slowly placed it over his eye. But the pain was too great and he immediately pulled it away.

"I told you it was going to hurt, but you need to put it over your eye and leave it for a bit." Then pointing south Elam added, "I'll be back in a while, I'm going after my horse."

Luke eased the poultice back over his eye, "You think they'll be back?"

"Oh, we'll probably see 'em again. Those Comanches ain't ones to quit. But it won't be here. If we see 'em again at all it'll be after we ride from here. They've already tried with ten and couldn't get the job done and now there's only four left. No sir, they may try to ambush us along the trail somewhere, but not here." Elam turned and walked away disappearing into the trees and thick brush just south of camp.

Luke looked west with his one good eye. The sun had set leaving only a dull red glow showing above the darkness of the distant horizon and he knew it was only a matter of time before that too would be gone. A pack of coyotes yelped a joyful howdy to the rising moon and somewhere in the distant north a lonely nightingale called to his mate.

It was well after dark when Elam returned with his zebra-striped dun. After stripping his gear he tied him among the boulders alongside the other horses. At the fire Luke had added jerked meat to the water that was boiling in a small pan. When Elam walked over Luke handed him a cup of hot coffee.

"My eye's doing a lot better," Luke said as Elam took the cup. "This here is the third poultice and it was making it feel so much better I found a string there in my saddlebag and tied it on." Luke paused then added, "We'll be in Sweetwater by late tomorrow or early the next day and if it's still giving me trouble I'll see 'bout gettin' some of that Doctor Black's Ointment to put on it."

"Never tried it myself," Elam replied, "but they say it's some mighty fine stuff." Then he pointed south. "Spotted something."

"What?"

"Campfire, mile and a half maybe two miles south of here—big one too—lots of flame. Whoever it is ain't caring whether anybody sees it or not."

"Logans," Luke guessed.

"Could be. Fire's a mite big for Injuns," Elam said sipping his coffee.

The night had started out warm with a light southerly breeze and had cooled a bit, but the wind had picked up and now blew steadily from the west. Clouds were building in the darkness and from time to time lightning could be seen. An eerie quiet fell over the prairie. Luke thought it was maybe too quiet because the few times he had been in a place where there was absolutely no sound it had meant trouble. It was a world without sound, none whatsoever—not even the flutter of an insect wing.

After dragging the two dead Indians down the hill to get them away from camp, Luke and Elam returned and had their fill of boiled jerky and beans. Elam dug his old slicker from deep within his bedroll and, taking his rifle, walked from camp along the bush line headed south. He had not said where he was going or if he would be back but Luke knew that such actions were not unusual for the old scout. He figured Elam was moving into the shadows to stand watch and he might not see him again until morning—even then it might be just long enough for Elam to have a cup or two of coffee, gather his horse, and ride out.

Luke had again soaked the bandana with the hot coffee and tied it over his eye. He walked from the fire and stood guard alongside the stone soldier on the northeast side of camp. He did not anticipate the Indians returning because like Elam had said, they had tried with ten and had not gotten the job done, and there were only four left—unless they rode out with the intentions of gathering more and coming back. Luke knew it was a strong possibility, because from what he had seen, this country was not short of Indians. There was also the campfire Elam had spotted, too. *Was it more Indians or the Logan brothers?*

Luke gently rubbed the folded bandana over his eye, found it still warm and his eye not nearly as tender to the touch as it had been—a sure sign it was getting some better. That in itself was a big relief for he knew without both eyes to spot where someone or something had stepped and left a track or broken a twig along the trail, or without the ability to notice a slight movement in the brush, a big part of his defense would be gone and that could lead to a deadly mistake or an ambush.

Suddenly, from the east came a light thumping sound. It wasn't much, but enough to get Luke's attention. He stood straight to look in that direction but, unable to see any more than an arm's length through the darkness, quickly turned an ear hoping to hear the sound again. For a long moment he stood motionless, holding his breath, straining to hear and see but nothing came from the darkness.

To the west lightning filled the distant sky and Luke could see the dark clouds still building and getting closer with each passing hour. Soon the rain would come, bringing vital moisture to this dry, parched land but, he knew too, also washing out many if not all the tracks left by man and beast. Not until the rains moved on and creatures moved again would the tracks reappear to provide a clue as to what and how many had made them, and in what direction they were headed.

A strange, uneasy feeling crept over Luke and for some unknown reason his mind told him not to move. Luke froze and remained perfectly still. He held his breath and listened, but after a few minutes of not hearing anything but his own heart beating, he slowly and without moving his head let his uncovered eye slide slowly to the right, then to the left. There was nothing to see but the black of night. For an instant, Luke thought about reaching up and removing the bandana from his injured eye in hopes of having better vision, but again his instincts told him to keep still.

For the next half hour Luke stood, not moving a muscle. Pain set in—the pain of numbness, especially bad in his legs and feet. *What harm will it do*, Luke wondered, *I need to move my legs to get the circulation back in my feet.* He tried wiggling his toes in his boots only to find he could not feel them.

For a good while longer he fought the urge to move, but the stinging pain kept growing until he thought he could stand it no longer. After giving his surroundings one more good listen and not hearing anything he slowly shifted his weight. Just as he started to move his right foot a sound from directly behind him stopped him cold. The rattling sound sent a chill up Luke's spine and caused the hair on the back of his neck to stand on end. Even in the coolness of the night, beads of sweat formed along his brow and within seconds were running freely down his face.

A rattlesnake had apparently crawled in next to the boulder seeking its warmth from the cool night, or maybe the little devil had moved from its resting place under the boulder where it had spent the day in the shade. No matter how it got there the rattler was now lying just inches from where Luke stood. He knew any sudden movement might cause a strike. He knew too, the tops of his boots had turned back the sharp fangs of rattlesnakes on many occasions before and would no doubt do it again if the snake struck from the ground, but if it slithered up on one of the many small ledges protruding from the boulder it might strike high, missing his boot tops altogether. Luke remained still and with the lack of movement the rattling subsided and once again the night was quiet.

Luke turned an ear toward the ground thinking he might hear the snake crawl away, but no sounds were heard. Even though he could not see, Luke was sure the snake was still near, ready to strike. He also noticed something good had come out of all the blood pumping excitement; his legs and feet did not seem to be aching anymore, and when he wiggled his toes he could feel them.

Lightning again lit up the night sky and a loud clap of thunder rolled across the heavens. In a hard gust of wind Luke heard the limbs high in the trees whipping and bowing against the force. Then the air suddenly filled with the sweet, clean smell of distant rain.

Luke needed to move. The rains were coming and he needed to dig his slicker from his bedroll, but realizing any movement might cause a strike from the rattler he remained still. He knew any snake bite would be bad, but one on the back of the leg would be the worst because it would be hard to see and even harder to tend. *I might be able to jump straight ahead and get clear before he can bite,* Luke thought, *but where there's one snake there might be two, and if I do jump I might jump right on top of the second one.* He decided to wait until either he was sure the snake behind him was gone or there was enough light to see the area around him.

Lightning streaked the sky, this time with a loud deafening crack and thunder that shook the ground.

There was a windy splatter of big, heavy rain drops followed by a lull and moments later, as if the sky had been ripped open, a downpour suddenly began.

Luke tilted his head so his hat would shield his face from the sting of the wind-blown rain, but felt something at his feet and slowly cast his one good, rain-blurred eye in that direction. When the lightning came again he saw the snake, seeking shelter from the downpour, had crawled to the ground between his boots.

The sight sent an instant rush of fear through Luke's body and he fought hard against the urge to jump away. With each passing minute the rain came down harder. Luke felt a light tap against his right leg, then another, and still another. When the lightning came again he looked to see the snake, trying to get away from the rising water, was trying to crawl up his leg. The sight almost made his heart stop.

An instant later in darkness, Luke felt the weight of the snake come down on his foot as it lowered back to the ground and started to crawl across the toe of his boot. When lightning lit up the sky again, Luke got his first good look at the deadly demon.

The snake's back was a good bit wider than a man's hand and when he finally did stretch out, Luke estimated him to be well over six feet long. A snake of enough size that a bite anywhere on a person would almost certainly mean the end, especially if the bite was in a spot where a man couldn't doctor it—like on the back of the leg.

Luke doubted the snake was really as big as it had appeared and knew that things seen in a flash of lightning looked bigger than they really were. Lightning could also make a man believe he saw something that was not even there. In the next flash of lightning Luke caught a glimpse of the snake's massive rattles as they disappeared beneath a little rocky ledge about ten feet away. Not knowing if that had been the only snake Luke did not make any sudden moves. Instead he took a deep, ragged breath and let it out slowly, then with his ears keen to the sounds around him, he slowly moved one foot. When the movement caused no rattling sound, he moved the other, and kept it up until he was turned and moving in the direction of the campfire. When he was clear of the boulders—and hopefully snakes too— he stepped quickly in the direction of the overhang but stopped to see if a snake might be crawled under it and bedded down. When he was satisfied none had, he ducked and went under.

He wasted no time stoking the fire, then hurriedly shook out of his wet clothes, put on dry ones from his saddlebag, and slipped into his slicker. Before long he was sipping a cup of coffee while enjoying the warmth of the fire.

From the heavens the rain and thunder continued and from time to time lightning would flash, lighting up the night sky. It was then, and only for a short moment, that Luke could see anything beyond the overhang.

Luke sat cross-legged with his Winchester lying at the ready across his lap, staring deep into the bluish-orange flames of the fire. He watched as they danced without direction along the newly-placed log and wondered what his beloved Loraine and Jack Elam were doing. For a long moment he sat motionless in thought, then a big lonely sigh escaped his lips. It had been such a long time since he had seen them. "It will be daylight soon," he said aloud and finished with a thought. *Then we can be on our way back to Sweetwater and then on to Rising Star.*

Lightning suddenly streaked the dark sky, and for that one split second, Luke looked out from under the overhang to see a blur that he thought for sure was an Indian darting in behind one of the boulders. In the same instant he heard what he believed to be a rifle shot echo from the not-too-distant south. Luke's body jerked and his pulse quickened at the unexpected sight and sound. The coffee cup flew from his hand as he scrambled to get to his knees and then to his feet. As he ran from under the overhang he reached up and ripped the bandana from over his eye.

With his Winchester leading the way, Luke moved with great caution through the rain and the night, hunkered down and moving one foot at a time as he made his way from one boulder to the next. The worst of the storm was over. The wind had died down to nothing more than a light, cool westerly breeze and the rain had become just a heavy sprinkle, but to the east lightning still flashed and thunder continued to roll across the sky. Beyond the wall of dark clouds, Luke knew the sun was starting to rise, but for the moment its golden rays were blocked from view.

Luke had worked his way slowly around and come from behind to where he thought he had seen the Indian. He was not disappointed when he did not see him, and was even a little relieved when he did not find the first sign that an Indian or anyone else had been there.

Still there was the gunshot, but that too might have just been a product of the storm and not a gunshot at all.

As Luke approached the stone soldier at the north-east corner of camp, night was giving way to the dim light of day. He slowed to have a good look along the ground for snakes, but not seeing any, quickly turned to look under the ledge where he knew for certain the snake had crawled. To his relief he saw nothing of the demon. He did, however, notice something that caught his attention. Down low on the ledge was a small amount of something with a dull, reddish color to it and he moved closer to get a better look. It was not until he ran his finger through the watery, red mixture and took it up to his nose that Luke realized it was blood.

"Blood from where?" Luke asked himself in a low voice. Then he thought, *Did the Indian that Elam shot in the neck somehow live through the ordeal and some-time during the storm sneak into camp for another try at taking the horses? If so, why had he made it this far and then decided against it?*

Again Luke glanced through the lightly falling rain at the quickly-disappearing spot of blood and wondered, had this blood been left behind by the Indian he thought he had seen during the lightning flash? If so, Luke knew it was also possible he had heard the rifle shot.

Suddenly from underneath the ledge came the loud, unsettling buzz of rattles and Luke, realizing his presence had once again disturbed the snake, quickly stepped back and had another thought. *Maybe the Indian he had seen had not been injured at all until he made the mistake of passing too closely to the ledge where that old rattler took a bite.*

With no answers to his questions, Luke turned from the ledge and moved from boulder to boulder working his way to where the horses were tied. By the time he got there the darkness had completely given way to the dawn and there was good light.

The wall of dark clouds continued to roll, and from deep within, lightning occasionally flashed, sending a bright, jagged shaft along the horizon. From time to time loud thunder shook the heavens.

Luke untied the horses and led them down the hill to a stand of grass where he put on the hobbles. At the overhang he positioned himself alongside the stone soldier at the southeast corner. He scanned the countryside, first along the brush line to the north, then east over the clearing and beyond, then finally to the south hoping to see Elam, but saw nothing moving or unusual.

I wonder where he's at, Luke thought. Then, imagining a good hot cup of morning coffee, he turned toward the overhand. The morning was quiet in the wake of the storm, with a light breeze blowing cool and damp from the west. Suddenly motion from above caught his attention and he looked skyward to see the early morning sky filled with hungry buzzards, some circling low with their wings spread wide. They had returned in full force.

Back at the fire Luke squatted on his heels, filled his cup, and took a taste. To the west countless birds chirped from the branches of a tall cottonwood where a squirrel clung to the trunk upside down fussing at another squirrel rustling among the dry leaves on the ground.

Hearing what he thought was the faint sound of a snapping twig, Luke grabbed his rifle and pushed away from the fire. Hunkered down, he quickly got behind the boulder. He held his breath and let his eyes search the thick brush all around and his ear turn in the direction he thought he had heard the sound, but for the moment the camp was again quiet.

"I must be hearing things," he said to himself in a whisper, but as he was rolling the situation around in his mind, he heard yet another sound from the same direction. This time Luke knew the sound because he had heard it many times in his life. It was the distinctive call of a Whippoorwill. He also knew that unless the bird had for some reason been flushed from its resting place it was almost too late in the morning to be hearing the call. He remained behind cover, his eyes searching because he had not heard a flutter of wings as he would have if the bird had actually been disturbed.

Luke glanced at the tall cottonwood noticing that the squirrels had vanished and the birds were no longer chirping. Only moments passed before the call came again, and Luke saw movement. Only when he realized it was Elam breaking from the brush did he ease the rifle to the bend of his arm and start from behind cover.

"I didn't know if you were going to show before I rode out or not," Luke said as Elam walked into camp.

"Been down the way a bit checking on that fire," Elam replied. Then he asked, "Got any coffee?"

Luke squatted and after filling a cup he handed it over, "What did you find out?"

"There's three wagons with four families in 'em headed west," Elam replied before taking a sip.

"West?" Luke questioned.

"Yes 'um, headed out Mexico way."

"Did you tell 'em there's not much water out that way?"

"Sure did. Told 'em that after they crossed the Colorado it got mighty scarce, but they've got two barrels on each of the wagons."

"Saw me another Injun last night during the storm, but didn't get a shot."

"Speaking of shot," Elam cut in, "someone let one go south and west of here. Did you hear it?"

"Yes I did, and I'm glad you heard it too, because I was startin' to think I was hearin' things."

"Don't know who," Elam explained. "All I know for sure is I heard one."

The two men finished their coffee then saddled the horses, loaded Pots Logan's body and stepped into leather. Looking over at Luke, Elam said, "If we don't run into trouble somewhere along the way I'll meet up with you in Sweetwater." Then spinning his horse he threw up a good-bye wave as he rode off in an easterly direction.

Luke watched him ride until he was out of sight and knew he would not see him again until trouble started or they reached Sweetwater. He knew too, that not seeing Elam did not mean he was not there. Touching Mousy with a spur he took to the trail leading south.

As he rode he thought that even with the best of luck, it was a long, hard day's ride from where he now was to Sweetwater, and that was with absolutely no trouble. Furthermore, they had killed only five, and wounded another of the ten Indians who had attacked them the day before which meant there were still at least four Indians who wanted their scalps running loose.

Those four knew where Luke was and what trail he was riding. If the Indians were not enough to worry about there was the gunshot he had heard during the storm—and he was now sure he had heard it because Elam had heard it too. Was it one of the Logans who had pulled the trigger?

"I don't know," Luke mumbled out loud to himself. Suddenly the strong smell of rotten flesh got his attention and he turned in the saddle and looked back in the direction of the dead man to find the still dripping, rain-soaked bedroll covered thick with flies. Turning back he fanned his hand at the fowl odor and focused on the western horizon, slowly searching for signs that would alert him to anyone watching nearby, to a plume of dust rising above the trees, a light wisp of smoke, or maybe anything moving on the horizon.

These signs would help him prepare in advance of an

attack. Suddenly he had an awful feeling deep in his belly—a feeling something was going to happen, and that danger lay ahead. *We don't have a chance of making Sweetwater today.*

Chapter Four

By mid-morning the sun burned brightly between the big, white, puffy clouds that drifted aimlessly across the pale blue sky. The trail was already hot, and what little air did move was heavy with a mugginess that was almost visible.

Despite the heavy rain during the night the ground had already dried and a thick cloud of dust rose under the horses' hooves as they made their way along the trail. A mile or so out Luke spurred Mousy across a creek that just a few days earlier had been bone dry. Now it ran pommel-deep to the horse and seemed to be rising.

Water stood in some low-lying areas, but other than those few puddles, a person would never have known the rain had stopped just a few hours ago. Topping a comb-like ridge, Luke stopped under the twisted, thorny limbs of a giant mesquite and for a short time sat quietly astride his horse looking back over his back trail. The buzzards he had left hungrily circling above camp this morning were now distant black dots though still circled among the low clouds off that way. But their numbers were fewer, leading Luke to believe many were now on the ground tearing at the flesh of the dead Indians.

Turning his attention west he saw the white of a distant *playa* and beyond it the "broken lands." Still further west great peaks reached high towards the heavens, bluish-gray with distance, cool and far away. Luke thought of the coolness of the peaks while drawing his handkerchief from his back pocket. He removed his hat and, after wiping the sweatband, ran his fingers roughly through his hair to shake out some of the sweat before slapping his hat back in place.

Eastward the gray of sun-baked plains shouldered against the blue of the mid-morning sky and the grass seemed to sway, but Luke knew the movement was not caused by the wind but by heat waves between the layers.

Stepping slowly to the ground he tied the horses to a low limb and loosened their cinches. It was cool in the shade but where shade did not exist the blistering, muggy heat remained. Luke thought about the coffee in his saddlebag and how good a hot cup would taste, and furthermore, of how good a warm poultice on his injured eye would feel. But not wanting to chance building a fire, he decided against it. Up to this point he had seen no signs that anyone was following him, but he knew it was not like Indians, especially Comanche, to let two white men get away with killing their people.

"No," Luke mumbled. *They'll be back. It's just a*

matter of time. There's no way they're finished with us yet. With that thought in mind he looked in the direction he'd be riding when he left the ridge.

His eyes searched along the tree tops for signs of rising dust or a wisp of smoke. He knew if the Logans did happen to come, they'd be riding from the south, and even though he'd seen no signs telling him otherwise, he had a God-awful feeling that sooner or later they'd show their hand. If they did, whether it was somewhere along the trail or later on in town, he wanted to be ready.

Looking further south, his eyes took in the outline of a far–off distant hill and he knew that just beyond it a few miles was the crossing at Sandy Creek. Then it was no more than five, maybe six miles due south from there to Sweetwater. But with the day already near half gone he also knew if he was going to get there before dark as planned, he needed to be riding. Turning, he made his way to the horses. After pulling the cinches tight, he swung up to leather, then giving his back trail one more quick look, he nudged Mousy with a spur and headed along the trail toward Sweetwater.

Some hours later and well south of the comb-like ridge and the coolness of the mesquite's shade, Luke rode tired and hungry. The only sounds were the steady clomping of the horses' hooves, the occasional creak of saddle leather, and from time to time a horse snorting to clear its nostrils of the suffocating dust. Just off the trail, and at the edge of a large patch of prickly pear, a butcherbird ate what remained of a small snake he had impaled on a cactus thorn.

In the not-too-distant south a crow squawked loud from its tree-top perch and Luke turned in hopes of seeing what had caused the disturbance. He reined in his horse, then standing tall in the saddle he let his eyes drift slowly over the area, knowing that more often than not a crow squawks at something moving—maybe nothing more than a coyote, or bobcat, but maybe at Indians, or the Logans, or possibly Elam riding through the brush.

The thought of the old cavalry scout being close to hand brought a sigh of relief, but at the same time Luke could not help but wonder why Elam had shown up in the first place. *Had Loraine asked him to come or had he taken it on himself after finding out the Tidwells had been so ruthlessly murdered?* Luke did not know, and he might never know the answer to that question, but he was sure glad Elam had come along when he did. Without his help Luke might not have lived through the Indian raid, especially with his eye injury.

But still he wondered. He had only known Elam Langtry for four years and the old man had already saved his bacon twice, once on Beaver Mountain, and again just yesterday. Of course Cork, Loraine, and Two Toes had had a big hand in his making it off the mountain too, because without each of them Roscoe Nash and his bunch of hired guns would certainly have killed all of them. And if not for Cork showing up when he did and pulling Luke out from under the barbershop in the first place Luke would not have survived the shootout with the McKuens in Rising Star.

To the two men Luke owed a debt he could never repay. He owed them his life not once, not twice, but three times. Luke could only imagine how any two men could be so much alike on one hand and so different on the other. From a distance one could hardly tell the two brothers apart. Their stature was about the same; both were tall, lanky, rugged men, with lean bodies and sloping shoulders, and even though Elam's hair was thinner and a bit longer, it was the same silver-gray as Cork's. Their faces, too, were a whole lot alike, thin and stern, leathered by the hot sun and wind, with deep lines of men up in years. They even had the same narrow, steel-gray eyes that seemed to smile from time to time. The only real difference between the two was in their nature.

Cork was a family man, easygoing and willing to listen to what a person had to say before taking action; still not a man who could be pushed around.

Elam on the other hand was a man who had, in his early days, ridden the North Country fighting Indians, and for several more years had been a top-notch scout for the cavalry. He had lived much of his life as a loner. He was a hard man with harsh ways, straightforward and to-the-point; a man who earned the respect of the folks around him with his fists and guns; a man who, once he got his mind set to doing something, was hell-bent on seeing it done.

Luke had heard of Elam long before they met, for Elam Langtry was known—as all such men are known—by reputation. Tales were told over campfires and around the trading posts and army forts by drifting cowhands and traveling salesmen and soldiers, and retold at saloons and gambling parlors. The stories of hard-nosed gunmen, relentless trackers and eagle-eyed scouts, of outlaws, crooked gamblers and of tough town marshals, were told until the mind of every man willing to listen was filled with legend.

It wasn't until Luke had seen Elam in action during those few days on Beaver Mountain that he realized the true stature of the man. Luke then realized that all he had heard about the old cavalry scout was most likely true.

One story told of Elam sneaking into a Sioux camp and escaping unseen with a white woman and her two kids whom the Indians had taken during a raid on a wagon train. Another tale was Elam single-handedly holding off more than two dozen Apaches, killing more than half of them in a period of five days while penned down in a buffalo-waller. Luke had also heard that Elam Langtry had once captured a half dozen wild horses and driven them into an Indian camp that was on the verge of starvation. Before leaving he even helped slaughter one of the horses.

But the story that Luke found hardest to believe was the one about Elam tracking four men who had robbed a supply wagon just south of Fort Collins, Colorado, all the way into Montana before catching up with them. Without firing a single shot, he reportedly returned all four, uninjured, to Fort Collins to stand trial.

No, Elam Langtry was not the kind of man who would give up on anything he set his mind to and he surely was not a man a person would want coming after him no mater what the reason. But he was a good, fair man and the right person to have on your good side if you needed help or if trouble started.

Suddenly from a thicket of scrub cedar about halfway up the next rise, Luke caught a glimpse of something moving. He drew up and stood tall in his saddle to have a better look and when he realized it was Elam his pulse quickened, because he knew if Elam showed himself so clearly it meant trouble.

Luke quickly let his eyes sweep the country in all directions but saw nothing that told him danger was near. Looking back to where he had spotted the movement he saw Elam sitting astride his horse facing west. After a while Elam slowly turned his horse left to face south, then a moment later spun the horse all the way around to the right until he was facing south again.

Luke knew what Elam was doing; he was using an old Indian trick to point out approaching enemies without using any direct movements of hand, making it almost impossible for anyone watching to know what was being done. Luke knew that the direction the horse's head was pointed when it came to a stop was the direction of concern.

If Luke was right, Elam was trying to say that trouble was approaching from the west and still more was coming from the south. The full circle Elam had made with his horse was to let Luke know he should swing east to ride around it.

Luke realized that he could not suddenly change direction because any such move would tip off anyone watching. He slowly continued due south for about half a mile; then at a large thicket of wild plum saplings he swung at a left angle around the cluster of thorny trees, but never turned back south.

After crossing a small grassy flat he rode into a shallow valley between two short rises, then dropped off into a dry, rocky wash and after about fifty yards turned back farther south. After he made the turn he heard what he thought to be a bird chirp but when he looked he saw Elam standing in an outcropping of large rocks. The zebra-striped dun lay flat on his side just a few yards away.

"They're fixin' to try to take us," Elam said as Luke drew up.

"Logans?" Luke questioned.

"No, sir," Elam answered dryly. "Indians. There's a half dozen or so west of here and at least that many if not more just the other side of that next rise yonder. They're back in the brush waitin'. I figure the ones to the west were goin' to see if they could maybe get after you and run you straight into the others."

Luke drew his Winchester from its boot and swinging his leg over the saddle slid quietly to the ground. "This looks to me like a good place to make a stand," he said while working the action on the rifle.

"You're right, Luke, this would be a mighty fine place if there wasn't a better one. But there is, and it's in that stand of oak along that ridge yonder," he said, pointing. "There's an old den of some sort, probably made by a mountain lion, it's no more than two, maybe three feet high but tall enough a person can get under it easy by laying down. It's been dug out under a thick slab of sandstone. It's 'bout halfway up and if we can make it there won't nobody be able to get to us from any direction but from the front-side, and for 'em to even try that they'll have to cross a little clearing."

Elam paused, then added. "They'll probably get the horses but that's a sight better than them gettin' our hair. If this thing works out the way I'm hoping it will, once we get to the ridge we'll have time to take the bridles off and put the hobbles on. Maybe that way they can't just ride in and lead 'em off."

"The horses and our guns are all they're after," Luke cut in.

"Maybe you're right, and I would have said the same thing before we killed those six or seven braves back yonder. But now things are a mite different . . . now you can almost bet they're huntin' scalp." Hearing a horse's hooves click stone, all talking and movement instantly stopped and both men glanced west at a single brave coming through the brush. He rode slowly with his eyes cast toward the ground. Looking back at Luke, Elam said in a low voice, "They've lost you, but it ain't goin' to take 'im long to find your trail. Then they'll all be coming." Motioning with his hand he added, "We can't ride straight for the ridge; there's a deep wash 'bout midway between here and there. It's hard to see until you get right up on it 'cause of all the tall grass, but believe me it's there—runs to within fifty yards or so of the ridge, ten or twelve feet straight down on both sides and a good fifteen feet wide.

"What we need to do is ride for that little cedar yonder and swing south just on the far side of it. But we don't need to go anywhere until those Indians on the south end start up this way. If we go too soon," Elam whispered, "they'll have an angle on us and will cut us off way before we get there."

With the plan set and the Indians getting closer the two men waited. Luke had untied the straps holding his saddlebags and moved them to hang over the pommel alongside the two canteens; he unlatched the rope and pushed Pots Logan's foul-smelling body from the extra horse. Now he stood with his hand over Mousy's nose to keep him quiet. Even though Luke could not see anything moving he did hear the horses' hooves clicking stone as they came from the south. Looking over to Elam he whispered, "Here they come."

"Get up old horse," Elam said in a quiet voice, and without anymore being said the dun immediately got to his feet. Both men slowly eased into their saddles and sat quietly, waiting for the right moment. When they heard the clicking stop, Luke put a hard spur to his horse and started in the direction of the cedar in a full run. He had no more than broken out of the wash when loud, ear-piercing war cries started behind them; then horses' hooves struck against rock and hard ground as the Indians started their pursuit.

"I'm gettin' too darn old for this," Elam called out as he leaned forward and double-slapped his reins.

Luke's mouse-colored horse took to the trail on sure, nimble feet; sidestepping rocks and mesquite, even jumping over a cactus, he ran with power and speed. Luke glanced over his shoulder to see the Indians had ridden from the rise and were coming fast but the distance had grown between them.

Raising the Winchester he took careful aim and slowly moved his finger over the trigger, then he applied light pressure, and after taking a deep, ragged breath, squeezed the trigger a little more, then a little more. The rifle suddenly leaped violently in his hands and before the recoil had eased one of the Indian horses in front tumbled head first, and the Indian hit the ground hard in a thick cloud of dust.

Another rifle barked loud and an Indian on a spotted pony threw up his hands and fell over backwards.

Three more times Luke fired and without looking to check the accuracy of his shots, he kept racing across the prairie toward the cedar.

With shrill yells and loud cries the Indians were still coming hard. At the cedar Luke suddenly swung south with Elam right behind him. As he turned, Luke emptied his rifle in the direction of the fast-riding Indians. Again one of the bullets found its target with deadly force but this time the Indian was close enough that Luke heard a loud pop when the bullet made contact. The Indian fell to the ground with a rolling bounce then quickly got back to his feet only to fall again.

Elam pulled the trigger on his Winchester two more times, and a spotted pony shied from one of the blasts, his rider swayed then fell spread-eagle into the sharp, thorny branches of a low mesquite.

Now riding to the ridge Luke fed shells into his rifle as fast as he could. When he looked back again the Indians had swung south to a better angle but in doing had turned too soon and were riding as hard as they could straight for the unknown danger of the wash.

"We should have it made now," Elam called out. But he had no more than gotten the words out of his mouth when an arrow struck, just missing his right leg, going deep into his pommel. He gouged the dun hard with his spurs and swung another double slap with his reins.

Luke glanced west and he could now see the wash well from where he rode and just as Elam had said, it was wide and deep, concealed completely from the west by the tall grass and obviously much too wide for any horse to jump and an instant death trap for any horse that fell into it. The Indians were still riding hard straight for the death trap.

With his loaded rifle, Luke pulled off another shot. As one of the Indians rode up to the wash, he drew his horse in hard but the animal was going too fast and as the horse left the edge the Indian lunged trying to jump. He made a good effort, but came up short and let out a loud, horrified scream as he fell to the bottom.

The second Indian drew in, but his horse slid just far enough that his front feet left the edge and, not being able to dig his back feet into the hard earth enough to stop, kept sliding. The Indian managed to jump onto the ground just as the horse squealed with fright and went over the edge.

Only the briefest moment passed before all the Indians had ridden upon the spot where the two horses had fallen into the wash. They whooped and hollered with their bows held high, then suddenly half turned back to the north, the other half south along the wash.

Luke knew those headed north would have to ride all the way back to the cedar and come around on the same route that he and Elam had taken. Those riding south, from what Elam had said, would not be able to cross the wash until almost reaching the ridge and the time that would take would hopefully allow the two men to hobble the horses and make their way up the rocky face of the ridge to the den.

"But what then?" he asked himself in a low voice. "Will they storm the ridge and try to take the horses in daylight? Or will they come at night under the cover of darkness?" Then another thought crossed his mind. *Maybe they'll just wait until we starve to death.*

Elam touched the dun with a hard spur and when he was alongside Luke he pointed, "There's the den. We want to leave these horses right out in front of it . . . there in that clearing."

Luke gave a nod and looking back saw the Indians still coming but at a distance of nearly a mile. Coming to the clearing he pulled Mousy to a sliding stop and stepped hurriedly to the ground. He quickly drew the hobbles from his saddlebags and slapped them on, then slipped the bit from the horse's mouth. After doing the same thing to the extra horse he unlatched the cinch on both saddles and pulled them off the horses. Loaded down with gear both men stepped among the rocks as they started the steep climb up to the den. With each labored step they took, the Indians were getting closer.

About midway Luke turned to see the Indians on the west side of the wash were closing in on the south crossing, and those who had ridden to the cedar were within a half mile. Time was running out and he knew it. Shifting his load Luke set his eyes on the narrow opening of the den and continued the climb.

It was hot and no wind stirred along the ridge. To the west the horizon was gray in the distance and the sun hung low and bright in a pale-blue sky broken here and there by wispy clouds that had no movement.

Above and far away a red-tailed hawk squelched loud as he effortlessly rode a current of air in search of food. Below the Indians were still riding hard from the west and north, and getting closer, their yells and war cries louder, their undying hatred for the white man growing, their need and hunger for blood pushing them beyond all else.

Taking the last few exhausting steps to the den opening Luke dropped his gear; then turning he let a quick shot go in the direction of the Indians coming from the north. The bullet fell well short of any target but close enough that the Indians slowed.

At the same time Elam put two better-placed shots toward the Indians coming from the west and both kicked up dust just a few yards in front of the horses. And as he turned he said again, "I'm gettin' too darn old for this."

They stacked the saddles in front of the opening and behind them placed the saddlebags and canteens, then got down on their bellies and, with their feet leading the way, slid under the overhang.

"How's your eye?" Elam asked as he settled into position. "I've seen turkey waddles in full season nowhere near that red."

"Still a mite sore, but I can see fine," Luke answered.

Below them the Indians were coming together and they all rode in a tight bunch at a distance they figured was beyond rifle range.

Elam threw his rifle over the saddle then flipped up the rear sight and slid the range-finder forward and rolled the lock. After taking a quick look he moved it forward a bit more, then looking over at Luke he said, "On the count of three, fire."

Luke gave an understanding nod and after a quick adjustment to the sights on his own rifle he looked over at Elam and said, "One . . ." He steadied the gun and brought the sights in line with the group of Indians. "Two . . ." He raised the barrel to where he could barely see the tops of their heads. Then he tightened his finger over the trigger and said, "Three." In the same instant both rifles belched lead and flame, and a thick cloud of smoke rose. The reports echoed off the back wall of the den with a deafening, earth-shattering roar and a moment later both men were being beaten by flapping wings as a dozen or so brown bats pushed past them and took to the evening sky.

Luke glanced back in the direction of the Indians to see they had scattered. Where they had been a spotted horse now lay still and about fifteen yards away an Indian struggled to move his feet then suddenly his senses gave way and he fell face down on the rocky ground and, like the horse, lay still.

"That's one less we'll have to deal with," Elam said while working the lever on his Winchester. "Good shot, Luke."

"Good shot yourself. I was just shootin' into the bunch hoping to maybe hit something."

Elam smiled, "At that distance that's all a man can do." Then turning around he looked as best he could into the dark den. "I hope that's all the bats . . . and I'm sure glad that old mama cat wasn't home."

Luke looked over. "Me, too. I believe I'd rather take my chances out here with the Indians than to crawl in here with a mad mountain lion."

Elam glanced back at the Indians to find they had moved north and were now well out of rifle range. "It'll be a while before they try anything else," he said with confidence. "When they come I'm looking for 'em to come up that draw yonder," he said pointing, "but on the other hand who knows, they may come straight at us. It doesn't really make any difference which way they come. 'Cause either way they'll have to cross that clearing." After taking time to think, he added, "That's what we've got to keep our eyes on, Luke . . . that clearing."

Luke gave an understanding nod, "I could make some coffee while we wait. It could be hours before they do anything.

"That might be a good idea. Who knows . . . when they do come they might have us pinned down for a good while. This might be our last chance to eat or drink anything for days."

"Speaking of eating," Luke said quietly, "my belly's so empty I can feel my belt rubbing against my backbone."

"My insides are gettin' a mite testy themselves," Elam replied. "I've got a bait of jerked meat here in my saddlebags and some coffee too, if we can get a fire started."

"Keep an eye on 'em," Luke said. Then crawling from the den he moved swiftly among the rocks gathering wood. His movements brought loud screams from the Indians below and two spun their horses and rode toward the ridge but they had not gone far when they were called back. Moments later Luke returned with an armful of wood and after dropping it behind the saddles he turned and headed out for more.

Elam readied his gun because he had the notion that when the Indians started the next time it would not be just one or two but the whole bunch, and they would not stop. The thought had not cleared his mind when loud screams and pounding hooves echoed as the Indians started again. "Luke," Elam called out, "You better step 'bout." Looking through the sights at the charging Indians he moved his finger over the trigger. He would wait until they reached the spot where the dead horse lay since his sights were already set at that distance. With sudden shuffling of feet and sliding rock Luke was coming fast with another load of wood.

"This should do it," Luke said, dropping the wood alongside the rest. Quickly dropping down to his belly he began working his way back under the overhang, but before he could get settled Elam's rifle roared sending one of the Indian ponies to the ground. The rider somehow landed on his feet and continued toward the ridge on foot. Elam's rifle spoke again but the bullet went wide of its target and struck only the ground kicking up a large plume of dark red dust. He quickly worked the lever again and fired, and this time the bullet found its mark. An Indian instantly grabbed at his horse's mane trying to stay on but he tumbled over backwards and landed head first on the ground.

Luke hurriedly drew his rifle over the saddles and pulled the trigger. Working the action as fast as he could he fired again and an Indian threw up his hands and fell from his horse. He slid another bullet into the chamber but just as he started to pull the trigger the Indians split into two bunches. One group rode west while the other swung east.

"They're going to try to get behind us and come down from the top," Elam called out. But just as he spoke the words two Indians broke from each group and rode toward the horses; moments later two more broke from each group and rode in the same direction.

Luke aimed for the Indian leading from the east but the bullet went low striking him high on the left leg.

Elam shot again and another Indian tumbled from his horse. Suddenly arrows began ricocheting off the rocks around them and the two men hunkered behind the saddles. When they looked out again the three remaining Indians had reached the horses. One rode up beside the dun and leaped onto his back while another slid to the ground, knife in hand. But as he bent down to cut the hobbles, Elam fired and the Indian flipped over onto his back and lay dead.

Another Indian mounted the extra horse and was kicking his sides, while the one Luke had wounded in the leg slipped a rope around Mouse's neck and was doing his best to lead him off. With their front legs hobbled the horses could only hop. Luke took careful aim and let fly a bullet in the direction of the wounded Indian; it found its mark with deadly force ripping at brown, naked flesh. The Indian instantly slumped forward, dropped the rope, and grabbed the horse's neck only to have that too, slip from his grasp as he fell.

More arrows bounced off the rocks around them and a few hit softer ground and went deep into the earth.

Elam's rifle roared again in the direction of the Indian sitting astride the dun but the bullet whipped past striking the ground. He worked the action again and pulled the trigger but this time heard only a click as the firing pin came down on an empty chamber. Elam reached for the box of shells and as he did Luke's Winchester sounded and the Indian let out a loud, agonizing scream and grabbed at the pain in his chest with both hands, then slowly slid from the horse and stood for a long moment with his arms draped over the dun's back.

Elam fed a bullet into the chamber and brought the rifle up but did not fire; instead he looked on as the Indian slowly turned from the horse and started walking away. "He's still moving," Elam said in a quiet voice, "but he's dead."

He slowly lowered his gun back to the saddle and watched as the brave man fought between life and death, and with the latter finally taking over, suddenly crumbled to his knees. As he started to fall forward, the Indian somehow flipped onto his back landing with his dark eyes cast toward the blue heavens.

Again loud cries echoed along the ridge and suddenly an onslaught of arrows rained down from all directions. "They've got us surrounded," Luke said.

"Yes, sir, they do and that's a fact," Elam replied. "We can't change that. But the only way they can get to us is to come straight up the hill and I'm a-thinking they ain't going to do that." Then looking at Luke he said, "Weren't you fixin' to start a fire? We might as well have a little coffee while we wait on their next move."

Without answering, Luke began breaking some of the smaller sticks and placing them in a pile near the den opening, then he added a few larger ones, and while he was starting the fire, Elam pulled the coffee pot from his saddlebags and dug around for the jerky.

To the west and only for the moment the sun's red glow dropped behind a thin line of blue-black clouds that lingered above the horizon streaking the brassy evening sky with finger-like rays of red, orange and yellow. Soon the array of colors would disappear and with them the last light of day.

Luke added water, then coffee to the pot and set it near the flames to heat, then let his eyes move slowly along the bottom of the ridge. The bodies of the Indians still lay where they had fallen, and not far away the horse and another Indian lay dead. The sight of so much death stirred an uneasy feeling in the pit of Luke's stomach, but he quickly realized that for him to still be alive this was the way it had to be. In this unforgiving land there were no second chances and only one firm rule that all western men were forced to live by, and it was a simple one. Do or die; kill or be killed.

"Here," Elam said as he handed Luke a piece of jerky. "It ain't much but it will give you somethin' to chew on."

Luke took what was offered with a thankful nod and then handed Elam a hot cup of coffee.

"It'll be dark before long," Elam said as he took the cup. After giving the hot coffee a cooling blow he took a sip and once it had settled on his insides said, "Now that's some mighty fine sippin'."

Luke looked over, "I'm not looking for any more trouble until first light."

Elam gave the statement some thought, then answered, "If they don't try something here in the next little bit I'd say you're right, Luke. And even though I have seen a few I've not seen many Comanches who like to move 'bout at night," Elam paused, then added, "After it gets dark I'm a-thinking 'bout maybe moving on down the hill a mite to where I can keep an eye on the horses."

"I'll go."

"No need in us both losing our hair. You just stay here and watch after the camp. But we will need to douse that fire before night comes." Elam took a long pull on his coffee. "They're on both sides of us, Luke and more along the top and though I'm not lookin' for 'em to be movin' 'bout after it gets dark, they will be somewhere close by watching—you can bet on that. In the last few days we've managed to beat 'em back but as you know, Comanche ain't ones to quit. No, sir, they're not done with us yet, and may not be until the last one of 'em falls."

A strong gust of wind stirred along the ridge and the flames spluttered under the coffee pot. Sand and smoke whipped under the overhang and Luke threw up a hand to shield his face. Instantly his injured eye began to sting and he quickly wiped at it with the back of his hand. A long moment passed before he tried to open his eye again and when he did the pain made it feel as though his eyelid was moving over a bed of gravel.

"Here," Elam said as he pitched the canteen, "you better rinse it out."

Luke bathed his eye until the painful grinding had subsided, then he pulled the bandana from around his neck, soaked it with coffee and gently placed it over his eye. There was immediately relief from the throbbing pain as he held it there.

The sun had dropped well below the horizon and a somewhat dull haziness had settled over the bottom. In the east a coyote howled at the rising moon and from the far north another cried back.

Luke rolled up on an elbow and took a stick to scatter the fire. The flames flickered, then faded into the smoldering black ash, a sporadic swirl of smoke disappeared into the dimness of the early night.

The den suddenly became dark with a blackness the eye could not penetrate. Both men sipped at their coffee and when Elam was finished he spoke quietly through the darkness, "I better be on my way." That said he took the rope from his saddle and started easing from under the overhang; once out he stood up and moved swiftly among the rocks, and as he went he made no sound whatsoever. Then he was gone as if he had never been.

Luke wanted desperately to sleep, to close his eyes and rest. His muscles and body ached from the long days and longer nights with no rest, and his eye hurt. He was as tired as any man with such little rest should be and to make things worse his belly was now contently full of coffee and jerky. But he could not sleep because he knew at any minute the Indians might show themselves and he must be ready—ready to shoot and kill.

To the north a lone star hung bright in the night sky and the moon's soft glow shone gray and dull over the ridge bottom. Again a coyote cried from a distant hill and his loneliness echoed along the ridge, but this time there was no answer or other sound.

Chapter Five

Elam moved slowly through the stillness of the night. He moved one foot at a time, placing each deliberately. Over his many years of tracking he had learned several things but the most important was to make no sound, be light on his feet, and breathe shallowly and steadily, taking in air only through his nose.

Even the slightest sound would carry a good way through the stillness of a prairie night and even moreso along a rocky ridge where sound might bounce from one rock to the next. He could not afford to make a sound because he knew the Indians were listening. If they had seen him leave the den they would be coming—and coming to kill him. He must, if at all possible, keep them from seeing him before he saw them, while at the same time moving downhill far enough to have the horses in view, in a position where he would hopefully have a slight advantage if they came.

And they would be coming either now or later Elam was sure. The Indians wanted the horses and wanted them bad. They wanted the guns too, but taking the guns would be easier if the Indians had control of the horses. All they would have to do is wait until Elam and Luke started out on foot, then ride ahead and set up an ambush along the trail.

Looking back up he let his eyes search for movement along the top of the moonlit ridge but saw nothing, and in the stillness of the dark night no sounds were being made. Elam studied the situation a bit longer and when satisfied he continued down the hill moving slowly and quietly. Though he sometimes had to feel his way among the rocks, with each step he was getting closer to the bottom and, even though he could not see the horses he knew he was close when he heard one of them snort.

Suddenly a pack of coyotes cried out in harmony and from the sound Elam figured the blood-chilling sounds had come from about where he and Luke had fired at the same time killing the Indian and his horse on the first charge. He glanced back in the direction he knew the opening of the den to be and knew it could be no more than twenty-five yards away, but with no light he could make out nothing more than the total darkness of the massive ridge.

With the rope in one hand and his rifle in the other, leading the way, he moved on down the hill another twenty yards or so to the last large boulder before moving clear of the ridge and standing still again to listen. Suddenly the night grew even darker as a cloud drifted between the earth and moon blocking its soft glow. The extra darkness made better cover for Elam as he moved toward the horses. When he came to each one he slipped the rope around his neck and took off the hobbles. When he had gathered all three he led them back to a little swag near the foot of the ridge. There he put the hobbles back on and dropped to the ground on his belly in among the horses with his rifle pointed westward in the direction of the wash where he figured the Indians would begin their approach.

Again the night suddenly came alive with the yapping cries of the feasting coyotes but once it had faded an eerie quiet returned to the land—a quiet that was broken only by the intermittent movement of the horses' hooves nervously stomping at the hard ground around him, and the faint thumping of his own heart.

The cloud had drifted past and the soft white of moonglow once again cast light into the darkness. Elam glanced through the night in the direction of the den but was again unable to see anything. Even though he could not see Luke he knew he was there. His eyes searched the night for any movement, and his ears were turned to the ridge, watching and listening as best he could for anyone or anything that might be coming down from the top.

As Elam looked again at the wash he thought back on how he had come to be where he was now. He had just returned from Beaver Mountain where he had spent the past several weeks helping Two Toes build a fence around the meadow north of the creek to keep his horses in close during winter. Before heading home the old Indian had given Elam a little beaded armband and small wooden tomahawk he had made for Jack Elam, and Elam, being the outstanding uncle he was, had ridden into town to deliver the gifts before riding on to the ranch.

Loraine had not asked him to come out here because it was not in her nature. But Elam could see the fear and worry in his niece's eyes and figured it would be best if he did. But it was not until he had talked to Slim Fathree, the deputy, and found out the Tidwells had been killed in cold blood for no apparent reason that he knew he should come out.

Before he left the jail it had become very clear that Luke was riding after killers of the worst kind, and possibly into something he could not handle by himself. Elam knew that anyone who could shoot down two old people in such a way would not hesitate for one moment to ambush someone else, especially a lawman coming to take away his freedom or his life—even moreso a man with the reputation of being as fast with his guns as Luke was.

Suddenly all three horses apparently heard something because their heads shot high into the air at almost the same moment. They stood on stiff legs with their ears perked and nostrils flared looking in the direction of the wash, and Elam knew then that something or someone was moving about. He slowly steadied his Winchester on his shoulder and moved his finger over the trigger. "Here they come," he whispered to himself as he strained his eyes. In the darkness there was nothing to see, and he heard no sound, but he was sure something was moving and he figured it must be Indians.

He waited patiently and watched, sweat running from his brow. He mopped at it with a sleeve. Surprisingly the horses suddenly turned their attention back to the ridge and before Elam could react a rifle roared from among the rocks and the report echoed with a loud, deafening crack. Before it had faded the wash was filled with the rustling of grass and intermittent crunch of dry leaves. Even though Elam could not see his hand in front of his face he could hear, and he took his first shot at the sound of moving feet.

Again the rifle above him spoke and a cry of pain filled the night followed by a faint thud and the scattering of pebbles as a body hit the ground. Hearing footsteps coming fast Elam pulled off a blind shot in their direction then, working the lever, he fired again. He heard a low moan followed by a loud gasp as the running turned into an off-beat stagger and with a brushy crash went silent.

On his right more footsteps moved through the grass and Elam drew the rifle around. At this angle he would have to shoot between the horses' legs and not wanting to take a chance on hitting one he started to stand to get a clearer shot. Just as he pushed up straight an Indian leaped astride the dun horse and in the same instant he swung with his tomahawk.

Elam ducked and as he did he pulled off a quick off-balance shot that missed wide just as the tomahawk made contact with his right arm knocking the rifle from his hand. The Indian let out a loud, ear-piercing war cry and came down hard with his right arm. The moon's soft glow reflected off a blade and Elam threw up his left hand to stop the plunging knife. With his right, he grabbed at the Indian's body to pull him from the horse. The rifle from among the rocks roared again as Elam threw the Indian hard to the ground. In an instant he was astride the Indian and they were locked in a fear-less hand-to-hand struggle for life that both knew only one would win.

The Indian was younger, faster and stronger, but the old army scout was smarter. When he felt the pressure on his hands lessen Elam released his grip and came across with a hard right to the Indian's chin and before the young brave could shake the blur of the blow Elam reached for the Indian's knife and in the next motion slipped the blade deep into his belly. The Indian flinched at the sudden pain and air spewed from his lips. One last, hard gasp for life failed and he was dead.

Hearing more footsteps Elam quickly spun, still on his hands and knees, and ran his hand over the ground in search of his rifle. Unable to find it he reached down for his pistol and just as the approaching Indian left his feet Elam pulled the trigger. Flame flashed in the dark night and the loud pop that followed told him the bullet had found its target.

The Indian let out a loud moan as the bullet ripped his chest and he landed with knife in hand on top of Elam forcing him hard to the ground.

Instinctively Elam pushed and kicked at the dead In-dian trying to roll clear of him but when he started to stand a terribly sharp pain mixed with a deep burning sensation down low in his side made any movement difficult. Slowly and with great care he pushed up on shaky legs with his pistol raised, cocked, and ready but he heard no more gunfire and no more footsteps. The burning pain grew more intense with each movement and he felt something warm running down his side but it was not until he reached down that he felt the knife handle.

He stood holding his breath for a long moment, his eyes searching the darkness, his ears straining with every fiber to hear, but he heard and saw nothing. After a bit he holstered his Colt and latched the leather thong over the hammer, then taking the bandana from around his neck he gritted his teeth against the pain, yanked the knife from his side and quickly shoved the bandana deep into the hole.

He stood leaning against the dun horse, grasping for breath, but knowing Indians were still out there slowly scooted his feet along the ground until he found his Winchester. He took cartridges from his gun belt and reloaded. The bleeding had slowed but not stopped completely, and Elam knew it was only a matter of time before the loss of blood would cause weakness to set in.

Sweat ran freely from his brow and his body shook as he fought the pain. Suddenly the world around him began to spin and for a brief moment Elam fought to re-gain control. But it was not to be and with his strength rapidly fading Elam dropped to his knees. As con-sciousness slipped away he slumped over face down, landing across the body of a dead Indian.

*   *   *

Luke sat between two large boulders no more than thirty yards uphill from where he knew Elam was, feeding bullets one after another into his rifle. He had heard the rocks slide as the two Indians made their way down from the top, but unable to see them he crawled from the den and had just gotten into position and brought his rifle to his shoulder when the Indian suddenly stood and drew his bow back to send an arrow flying in Elam's direction. When he stood the moonglow lit up his outline. The impact of Luke's shot sent him to the ground and the arrow in a harmless unguided direction.

It had taken time for Luke to find and kill the other Indian and he might not have found him if his bow had not lightly scraped a rock giving away his position.

With his rifle loaded Luke eased it into the bend of his arm and leaned back against one of the boulders. As he did he wondered if his good friend Elam Langtry was still alive. Luke had heard several shots and countless screams from below indicating there were many attackers and he could only hope that Elam had somehow been able to survive. He also wondered if the horses had been taken. He had not heard the sounds of any horses being ridden off as he would have if the Indians had gotten them. He knew he could neither take the chance of moving down the hill to find out nor call out. If there were still Indians nearby he would surely give himself away.

Luke looked east and the haziness told him it was nearly morning. He would then be able to see and would know if the old army scout had been killed. For now he would be best served to sit quietly and wait. Atop the ridge a whippoorwill called and moments later another answered from the wash. As much as it sounded like whippoorwills, Luke knew it was most likely the Indians signalling one another.

Unexpectedly a persistent itch spread through his beard and he scratched it, and as he did he thought of his razor. He needed to shave, take a bath, and change into fresh clothes and knew it would make him feel and smell a sight better.

Suddenly his nostrils filled with the unmistakable aroma of lilac. He wondered about its origin but quickly realized that the pleasant scent was only in his mind—a distant memory of a happier time. Then his mind filled with thoughts of his beautiful Loraine, the softness of her skin and the smell of lilac in her freshly washed hair, and he smiled.

The whippoorwill call came again from along the top of the ridge and as before an answer came from the wash, but this time both seemed nearer. *They are getting ready to try again,* Luke thought as he quickly shifted his weight and brought up his rifle.

In the east the first glimmer of light was spilling over the horizon as the sun began its slow, steady climb toward the heavens. Soon there would be enough light to see and then the Indians would come. How many and from what direction Luke did not know; he only knew he had to be ready to do whatever was necessary to save his own life.

Over the past few days the Indians had taken an awful beating. Many lay dead and several more had been wounded, both here and back where the stone soldiers had stood guard. But Luke knew it was not like Indians to give up just because one or two had died and he figured that at first light they both—if Elam was still alive—were in for another long, hard day.

With each passing minute the night was growing hazier with the coming of morning, and from behind the eastern horizon a massive glow was building. Luke slowly let his eyes search along the ridge as its roughness began emerging from darkness but it was still too dark to distinguish between rock and man.

Then, as every day starts, so started this one with just a ray or two as the sun began peeking over the tree tops in the east. Then it rose a little more, and still more until the outer edge of the giant ball of fire came into view. Within moments its golden rays streaked the far-off cloudless sky pushing the long shadow of the ridge and all that stood around it long and jagged to the west.

Luke rubbed the watery crust from his injured eye and quickly glanced along the ridge but after seeing nothing unusual he turned his attention to the bottom. There he saw the dim outline of the horses standing in a tight bunch near the foot of the ridge, all with their heads high in the air. His eyes moved slowly over the dead quiet of the gray bottom resting on each bush and rock for a good close look before moving to the next. The old scout was nowhere to be seen and there appeared to be no movement.

Suddenly one of the horses whinnied and when Luke looked back he noticed what he thought might be a body sprawled on the ground among the horses. Luke rose to his knees so he could better focus his eyes through the dim morning light and when he realized what he was looking at an uncontrollable sick feeling washed over him. It was a body alright, and not one but three. Two of the bodies were clearly those of Indians, but the other, the one dressed in buckskin, was Elam Langtry. Luke was certain.

Before he could give the death of his friend and wife's uncle much thought, movement along the ridge drew his attention and he looked back just as a half-dressed brown body dropped behind a rock. Further up the hill still another Indian was on the move, hunkered down with an arrow notched in his bow.

Luke looked back at the bodies and knew that with Elam dead the only chance he had to survive the upcoming attack was to somehow get back to the den and even then survival would only be luck because with no way to escape all the Indians had to do was wait him out. There was not much water left in the canteens and what little food remained in the saddlebags would last only a day or two at best. With Elam dead there was no possible way that Luke could hold off this many Indians by himself; it would only be a matter of time before they would have the horses. *Maybe then,* he thought, *they'll consider it a victory, gather their dead and ride out. On the other hand maybe if I can get to old Mousy we can outrun them. He's had plenty of rest and it can't be more than five or six miles to Sandy Creek. I doubt, even though they'd like to have my scalp, that they'd pursue me beyond there.*

Luke glanced in the direction of the horses and judged the distance at forty yards and for most of the way there were rocks for cover. Looking back at the Indians coming down from above he decided that to out-run them was his only chance. He would have to kill these first two and hope there was not a passel more in the wash who could cut him off from the horses.

Knowing what needed to be done, Luke drew deeply from his well of courage and brought his rifle to his shoulder. At that moment he thought of Loraine and Jack Elam but his thoughts were cut short when he looked down the sights and saw the Indian looking back in his direction.

The Indian rose quickly to his feet with his bow drawn back. At that moment the rifle bucked and smoke and lead belched from the muzzle. The bow flew from the Indian's hand as he tumbled backward and disappeared into an outcropping of rocks.

Luke heard a loud swoosh then a click as an arrow passed within inches of his head and struck the boulder beside him. He spun to see the other Indian had come from behind his cover and was notching another arrow. Luke worked the lever and the Winchester spoke again, the impact of the bullet driving the Indian back against the rocks where he stood for a brief moment with his eyes locked on Luke's. Then his legs gave way and he slowly slid to the ground leaving a bright red smear of blood on the rock.

Luke quickly jumped to his feet and started for the horses at a full run. At the same instant war cries filled the early morning air from the top of the ridge and the wash as the Indians charged. Luke had not gone far when the first Indian broke through the brush and into view and almost instantly a rifle at the bottom roared and the Indian threw up his hands and fell. Elam stumbled to his feet and pulled off two more quick shots, then turned in the direction of the den.

Upon seeing his old friend still alive but moving slowly Luke drew up behind a boulder and fired several shots as quickly as he could, hoping to slow the charging Indians. It was evident when they dove for cover that his plan had worked.

With each step Elam was getting closer to cover, but he was holding a hand to his left side and dragging his leg. Obviously he was in a great deal of pain and was struggling just to move his feet.

Luke glanced toward the top of the ridge to see two more Indians working their way through the rocks but neither was quite within range.

Twenty yards away Elam stumbled and fell to the ground but slowly got back to his feet and staggered on.

The Indians from the wash started again and Luke pulled off a shot dropping the first. "Come on," he called out to Elam.

"I'm coming . . . I'm coming," Elam answered in a broken voice.

"What happened?" Luke asked as Elam moved in behind the rock.

"Injun got me last night," Elam answered while trying to catch his breath, "and got me good, too."

"I can see that," Luke replied pointing to Elam's blood-soaked shirt and pants. Then he asked, "Can you make it on up to the den?"

"I reckon I better make it if I don't want those varmints gettin' my hair."

Luke motioned with his gun barrel, "You go on up but watch out for the two coming down from the top, yonder. I'll see if I can hold these off a bit longer."

Elam started up the hill but the loss of blood had sapped much of his strength and the steep incline made moving very difficult.

The Indians from the wash charged again and this time there were at least a dozen if not more, and it did not look as though they had any notion of stopping. Luke killed two with three shots and wounded another; then, just as he turned to move uphill, Elam pulled off a shot and one of the two Indians coming down from the ridge top threw up his hands and tumbled.

"Let the Indians get right up to 'em then shoot at the dun's feet," Elam screamed out.

"Do what?" Luke called back.

"When the Indians get close, shoot at the dun's feet."

Not understanding but not having time to question, Luke raised his rifle and took careful aim. When the Indians were no more than five yards from the horses he pulled the trigger.

A big cloud of dust kicked up just under the dun's belly and he shied away from both the sudden noise and the approaching Indians. Then spinning as though a bear were after him, he took off and since they were all tied together the other two horses went with him. Apparently Elam had taken off the hobbles because they were all in full stride.

Elam let out a big hoot and holler. "That dun's the best damn horse in this country! I'd rather see him dead as to see an Injun on 'im."

Luke smiled and turned to make his way to the den,

but with less than thirty yards to go another Indian came from behind cover and let an arrow fly. Luke dove and the arrow missed high. While still on the ground he pulled the trigger and the bullet hit the Indian's head; he was dead before he hit the ground. Quickly getting to his feet Luke moved up the hill and reached the ledge just as Elam was sliding under.

"They're going to get the horses," Luke said.

"Maybe not," Elam answered. "They're going to have to catch 'em first and that dun, let me tell you, Luke, likes Injuns less than I do. I just hope by 'em being tied together the way they are, they don't get hung up on a tree . . . and they get far enough away that the Indians don't find 'em."

The two men threw their Winchesters up over the saddles, pulled the triggers, and both shots found their targets. Suddenly the Indians stopped and took cover. "They made a mistake lettin' us get back to this den and they know it," Elam said. "They won't come any further. Hell, they ain't crazy enough to try coming up that hill in the daylight."

For a long while there were no sounds and no signs of movement by the Indians from above or below. All of a sudden one called out to the others and moments later started moving back down the hill, being careful not to show too much of himself.

Not long after he disappeared back into the wash the rest followed one at a time until they were all gone. "That's it for a bit," Elam said through gritted teeth. Then grabbing at the pain in his side he said, "I've had worse, but that was a good many years back."

Luke looked over, "How bad is it?"

Elam shook his head, "I couldn't tell in the dark, but the knife went deep, I could sure tell that when I pulled it out," then motioning with a hand he said, "If you don't mind, Luke I'd be obliged if you'd have a look. We may need to sew it up. I've got a needle and thread there in my saddlebag."

Luke leaned over to have a look and what he found under Elam's shirt sent a cold shiver up his spine. There was a jagged two inch long gash down low on Elam's left side just above his hip-bone. The knife had gone deep but on an angle and in a place where no organs were hit. "My goodness, Elam, is this little old thing here what you're whining 'bout?" he asked playfully.

"What do you mean, little old thing?" Elam growled. "That there's enough to kill most men." Then he saw the smile on Luke's face. "Why you . . . I should have let Roscoe Nash or the McKuens have you." Then he laughed and asked, "What do you make of it?"

"It's full of dirt so we'll need to clean it up," Luke answered. "If we can get the hole closed I think you'll be alright. You're going to be sore for a few days but you'll live." Luke turned back toward the opening and then, breaking a few of the sticks he'd plied up the day before, he started a small fire and after filling a pan with water he set it over the flames.

He caught movement out of the corner of his eye and looked into the bottom to see several of the Indians had gathered well north of where the Indian and horse lay dead and well out of rifle range. "What are those devils up to now?" he asked. But the words had no more than left his lips when a horse and rider broke from the brush on the west side dragging something tied to a rope. Luke looked closer and realized the object being dragged was Pots Logan's dead, rotten body. It was still wrapped in the bedroll and if it had not been, Luke was sure it would have come apart.

"Don't pay 'em no mind," Elam said. "They're just stirring up dust. They may be trying to get our attention so a brave or two can work their way down from the top. If that's what they've got in mind let 'em try, but they already know as well as we do it ain't going to work. But if they really want to . . . let 'em try, and we'll leave more Indians laying dead."

When the water had boiled Luke cleaned the wound. After threading the needle he asked, "You ready?"

Elam gave a nod; then, placing a stick between his teeth, he clamped down.

Luke eased the needle through the skin on one side of the wound, and Elam's body flinched but from that moment on he lay still, not even making as much as a wiggle. In no time the hole was sewn closed; Luke pulled an old shirt from the saddlebags and wrapped the wound. "There you go," he said, "I ain't no doctor but the hole's closed up tight and the blood's stopped."

Elam gave a thankful nod, "I'd say you did a mighty fine job. The one here on the other side," he said pointing, "I had to sew up myself. It was from an Indian lance. Just as the Indian threw it, I pulled the trigger. He never knew it hit me. Went all the way through, it sure did, and pinned me to the trunk of an old cottonwood. I stayed that way for the better part of two hours before I worked up enough nerve to pull it out." He shook his head. "I'm gettin' too old for all this shootin' and stabbin' and sewin' things up."

"It can really start showing on a body after a bit," Luke answered.

Elam slowly rolled onto his belly and then, looking over the saddles, he asked, "How many you reckon we've killed?"

"I don't rightly know—a good many of 'em I'd say."

"Why do they keep comin' knowing they're going to get killed? For those three old horses? No, sir, it has to be more than the horses. It has to be somethin' inside of 'em."

At the bottom the whooping and hollering continued, and Pots Logan's body was still being dragged back and forth. When one horse would get tired they'd switch and another would drag him for a while.

Luke and Elam lay in the den watching quietly while sipping coffee. The cloudless sky was filled with buzzards. Many had landed in trees and several more at the dead bodies, squawking and flapping their long, black wings as they ripped at the flesh of man and beast.

Luke flipped up the back sight on his rifle, "I've had about enough," then sliding the range-finder up to the last notch he locked it in place.

Elam glanced over, "That would be one hell of a shot."

"Doubt if I can hit anything, but maybe I can get close enough to let 'em know we're still here."

"Well wait for me. It might have more of an effect if we both do it at the same time. Tell you what . . . Do you see that one sittin' there with those four or five by that mesquite? The one on that shabby-looking spotted pony?"

Luke nodded his head, "On the count of three. You ready?"

Elam nodded back as he brought the rifle to his shoulder then let it rest across the saddle. He knew that if such a shot hit anything it would be complete luck; on the other hand it might hit and if it did there would be one less Indian to deal with.

"One . . ." Luke said as he brought the front and back sights in line with the Indian sitting atop the spotted horse. "Two . . ." he raised the front sight to where he could barely see the top of the Indian's head. "Three," he pulled the trigger. Both Winchesters barked at the same instant and the den filled with smoke. It was several seconds before anything happened but then two puffs of dust kicked up just a few feet in front of the group of horses and they spun away. The abrupt movement made the Indians grab the horses' manes to stay on but one reacted a bit late and went off the side hitting the ground hard.

The spotted horse reared and flipped over backwards onto the rider, and another started bucking. The buzzards at the dead bodies squawked and took wing and the rest of the Indians scattered. The one dragging Pots Logan's body fell in behind a rock for cover.

"Hell of a shot, Luke," Elam shouted with a laugh, "we didn't hit anything but we came awful close . . . close enough to put some fear in 'em. Now I reckon they'll move on back a mite further."

Luke smiled at Elam's excitement; then, hearing a

loud holler, he looked back toward the bottom. The Indians had gathered again but this time at even a greater distance. They sat studying the situation a good while, then one rode out from the bunch to look at the ridge; after a bit he returned and said something to the others, then turned to face the ridge again. He sat for another good long bit just looking, trying to figure out a way. Finally he realized what Elam and Luke already knew. The only way in was straight up the front and their last such attempt had already proven deadly.

All of a sudden he raised his bow high above his head and called out. Moments later the top of the ridge came alive with the sound of horses' hooves clicking stone as they began to move out; before long they broke from the wash and rode to meet the others in the bottom.

Again they sat looking at the ridge and from time to time one would let out a loud war cry and start his pony at a full run but draw up short of rifle range.

"Well I'll be darned," Elam said looking over at Luke. "They're going to give it another try." Reaching, he threw open the flap of his saddlebag and pulled out a box of shells putting it directly in front of him so it would be within easy reach. He had no sooner done that than the lead Indian turned and rode in among the others; after a short pause he put a hard heel to his horse and rode north. The others sat whooping and hollering and waving their bows in the air. Then they too turned and followed their leader.

"They're quittin'," Luke said. "They've had all they want."

"It sure looks that way," Elam replied. "But we don't want to go jumping the gun too soon."

The two men lay watching as the distance between them and the Indians grew and moments later the Indians rode over the northern horizon and disappeared.

"Well now, don't that beat all?" Luke said, as he started crawling from under the ledge.

"You best watch yourself," Elam called after him. "They're sneaky varmints. One or two might have stayed behind."

Luke stood, then slowly let his eyes search in all directions, but other than the buzzards squawking and circling overhead there was nothing moving anywhere and no other sounds to be heard. "They're gone," Luke said after a bit.

Elam extended his hand, "Here, help me up." Once out on his feet Elam turned from the ledge, then placing two fingers in his mouth he spread his lips and let go two loud whistles.

Not understanding, Luke asked, "What was that for?"

"Oh, nothing really," Elam replied, "just seein' if my whistler still works." In the back of his mind he was hoping the dun had heard the whistle and if he had Elam knew he would come running. The only thing that would keep him away was the rope hung up on something or the Indians, if they had him.

Luke shook his head, then started from the den.

"Where you going?" Elam asked.

"I'll be back in a bit."

Before long Luke returned carrying a good-sized

mesquite limb that forked on one end, and after working on it with his knife he handed it to Elam and said,
"Here, you can use this limb as a crutch. It will be better than trying to use your rifle and gettin' dirt in the
barrel."

"Much obliged. But I don't think I'll be needin' it."
Then taking his hand up to his mouth he gave two more
loud whistles. When nothing happened Elam seemed to
grow worried. Again he whistled and again nothing
happened.

Elam eased over and took a seat on a nearby rock
where he had been sitting only a short time when from
the east came a faint, distant sound, then another and
still another until it was clear that the sounds were
hooves clicking stone. He glanced at Luke with a big
smile on his lips and only moments later the dun, still
leading the other two horses, walked into view. "Told
you, Luke, that dun mustang there is the best horse in
this here country . . . and the funny part is I stole 'im
from an Injun."

"I see it," Luke replied, shaking his head in astonish-
ment, "but I wouldn't have ever believed it."

Elam took up his Winchester and with the help of the
crutch started the long descent to the bottom. While he
made his way down, Luke saddled the horses, and rode
out to see if there was enough of Pots Logan's body left
to drape over a saddle.

The bedroll was ripped in a couple of places but considering what it had been through it was still in fairly
fine shape. Luke tried holding his breath while loading
the badly decayed body but he did not get it done be-

fore he was forced to take a breath and the awful smell turned his stomach. "That's what I get for killing 'im," he mumbled while gasping for fresh air. With the body loaded Luke crawled into the saddle and rode back to the foot of the ridge where Elam waited. "Can you ride?" he asked stepping to the ground.

Elam gave a nod, "If you'll give me a hand up. I've tried but that stirrup seems to be a goodly way off the ground."

Slowly Luke helped Elam into the saddle, then swung up to leather himself, and with the sun hanging high in the cloudless sky, they turned and headed south.

They rode slowly because of the pain Elam had to endure and they stayed to the brush as best they could because both men knew that the Indians' riding off did not mean they were gone, or would not be back. Even if the Indians were gone, Luke knew the Logans might be out there.

Chapter Six

Luke rode in front leading the horse carrying Pots Logan's dead, rotten body. His eyes were constantly on the move, searching the trail in all directions near and far for any signs of Indians or the Logans. He rode with his pistol loosened in the holster and his rifle across the pommel.

They had traveled little more than two miles from the ridge when Elam suddenly drew up; he slumped in the saddle without speaking. His face was pale, his hands shook, and he was breathing in hard, uneven gasps.

Luke sat awaiting some word but when he got none he looked over and asked, "What's wrong Elam?"

"I'm not feelin' up to snuff." Elam replied and after a half-hearted attempt at wiping the paleness from his face he added, "My leg's hurtin' awful bad, Luke. And I've got a hard knot the size of my fist where that knife went in. I can hardly bear the pain sittin' here on this horse."

Luke knew Elam Langtry to have an enormous tolerance to pain and his saying anything meant there had to be something severely wrong. No doubt, the agony he was suffering had already gone well past what most men could have endured.

Luke quickly stepped to the ground. "Let's have a look," he said as he reached up to help Elam from the saddle. Raising his shirt Luke saw the big, black knot that had welled up around the gash where the blade of the knife had entered. Luke shook his head, "There's something in there that's come loose, Elam, and you're bleeding on the inside. There's nothing I can do without opening you back up and then I don't know that I could do anything to stop it. You need a doctor."

Elam raised his head and after taking a long look in all directions he focused his eyes back on Luke and said, "You're the closest thing I see to a doctor around here." Then motioning toward the injury with a hand he asked. "Can you maybe stick a hole through the skin there someplace so the blood can drain?"

Luke nodded his head, "I can, but that might not be the smart thing to do. Letting the pressure off might cause it to bleed more. If you think you can tolerate the pain we might be better off to leave it alone for now and try to get you on into Sweetwater."

"I don't know if I have it in me to get back in the saddle."

"You're not gettin' back in the saddle," Luke answered. "You need to be on your back. I'll put together a travois, that way you can lay down."

"No need going to all that trouble. Maybe I can try riding with my right leg turned back over the pommel. Surely that would take some of the pressure off."

"No trouble," Luke replied. "If I remember correctly not long ago you did the same for me." That said Luke mounted and rode in the direction of a little stand of cottonwoods atop a short rise just a couple hundred yards to the east. He returned a short time later with two long cottonwood saplings. Taking Elam's rope he attached the poles to the saddle on the dun horse, then taking the rope from his own saddle, Luke weaved it between the two poles and put Elam's bedroll over the top.

To the north the ridge was purple with distance and above it buzzards dotted the blue midday sky. Each circled with wings spread wide waiting a turn to land, eat, and clean up the death that the brutal hostilities of man had left behind.

"You ready?" Luke asked extending a helping hand to Elam.

"As ready as I'll ever be," was the answer.

With Elam loaded they started along the trail heading south. For the most part the travel was dusty and slow and in places rough but by mid-afternoon they topped a little rise; at the bottom was Sandy Creek. Its waters ran slow and shallow among the rocks and after dipping a cup for Elam, Luke dropped to his belly and drank the cool, clear water. Finally he stood and mopped his mouth with a sleeve and then after stripping the gear from the horses he let them drink. When they had their fill he led them to a small stand of oak where the grass grew tall, thick, and green. There he put on the hobbles and the horses immediately dropped their heads to graze.

On his way back to where Elam lay, Luke gathered wood enough from a cottonwood deadfall to start a fire. After adding water to the coffee pot, he set it over the flames; pouring more water into a pan he set it near the flames to heat. Then he went back to the creek and filled the canteens.

When the water in the pan was warm, Luke bathed Elam's wound. Then he filled two cups with the hot coffee and, taking what little jerky that remained from the saddlebag, he offered it to Elam. He waved off the jerky but took the coffee with a slight nod of thanks and a half-hearted smile.

"We'll rest here a while, then head on," Luke said as he took the cup up to his mouth. He knew it was still another eight maybe ten miles to Sweetwater and at the rate they were going they would be lucky to get there by first light—if everything went well. Elam's wound looked bad and the black knot continued to grow larger with each passing hour as the blood leaking some-where inside his body continued to pool. His face seemed swollen and he had a dull, reddish tint to his cheeks probably due to the onset of fever. For the past few hours he had been having mild bouts of what seemed to be delirium when he would drift in and out of consciousness.

Luke knew he could probably lance the knot and the blood would drain but in doing so he might also release the pressure that might be keeping Elam from bleeding to death. On the other hand he could open him up and sear whatever it was bleeding. He looked at his old friend to find he had dozed off and the coffee cup lay empty on the ground where it had landed after slipping from his hand.

With no time to waste, Luke hurriedly saddled the horses and mounted, giving Mousy an easy nudge with a spur across Sandy Creek. As they broke over the top on the far side Luke turned his attention west to see the sun hung low in the brassy sky and knew that night would soon be upon them. He knew, too, that Elam Langtry was most likely dying from his wound and the only chance he had—if he had any—was to get him to the doctor in Sweetwater.

Tired and hungry Luke rode on through the dim light of evening, and after the sun dropped behind the horizon he continued through the dead dark of night, stopping from time to time only to check on Elam and give the horses some rest.

Three miles back he had ridden up on a wash that he had crossed without any trouble when going north; but with the travois there was no place that was not too steep to cross and they had lost an hour or better riding around it.

Suddenly the stillness of the cool night was filled with a loud agonizing moan; Luke looked back to see Elam wildly kicking his feet and flailing his arms high in the air. Luke drew up and slid to the ground in a run and got to his old friend just in time to keep him from flipping from the travois. "Hold on there," Luke said.

Elam opened his eyes wide and yelled, "Get 'em off me . . . get 'em off me!"

Luke frantically slapped at Elam's shirt thinking something was biting him but in the dark he could not see. "Get what off?" he asked. Elam did not answer and there were no more moans; the old scout lay quiet.

Luke slowly placed his hand on Elam's forehead to find it hot to the touch and when he raised his shirt to check the knot, he found his clothing dripping with sweat. "He's burning up," Luke mumbled to himself. He quickly made his way back to the horse and took the canteen from the pommel; after soaking his bandana in the cool water he bathed Elam's face, then placed the wet bandana across his forehead.

Stepping back into the saddle Luke moved out knowing that time was slowly but surely running out. The thought of Elam dying sent a cold chill up Luke's spine for he knew that, if not for him, Elam would not have gotten stabbed; if not for him, Elam would still be in Rising Star or up on Beaver Mountain visiting with Two Toes; if not for him.

Two hours further along the trail Luke drew up on a hill covered with giant oaks and again checked Elam's condition. As before he washed Elam's face and afterwards placed the cool, wet bandana back on his forehead. Then they moved on south.

The sun was just starting its long climb for the heavens when Luke drew up again. Golden rays lay softly upon the land and all that grew upon it ever so gently. But with a force not to be denied those first few flickering rays pushed and shoved the darkness bringing the light that marked the start of a new day and welcoming warmth to the cool morning.

Luke slid slowly to the ground and after giving Elam a quick check and finding him still breathing, he bathed his face and placed the bandana back on his forehead, then back in the saddle he rode on, knowing he had to be getting close. He did not realize just how close until he rode over the next rise and the little west-Texas town of Sweetwater came into view.

At that moment a big smile came to Luke's tired, bearded face and a great sigh of relief rolled from his lips. He nudged Mousy on but it was not until he started along the wide dirt street that he really believed he was there, and that help for his old friend was just minutes away. He turned and looked back in the direction of the travois but could not tell from that distance if Elam was alive or dead. He was not moving or making any sound.

Doors swung open all along the street and the town-folk ran from the buildings out onto the boardwalks. The town suddenly sprang to life as people stepped into the street from all directions and fell in behind the horses hauling the dead and injured. Coming to an old man standing near a hitch rail, Luke drew up and asked, "Have you got a doctor in this town?"

The man pointed to a big, white house surrounded by a freshly-painted picket fence and answered, "Yes, sir, and a good 'un. That's his office yonder."

Luke gave a nod, then pitching the lead rope to the horse carrying the remains of Pots Logan he said, "If you would please, sir, see that this killer gets to the undertaker."

The man took up the rope, then looking back at Luke he answered, "Yes, sir, I will. But who is it?"

"That there is what's left of Pots Logan. He's got a few holes in 'im and he's missing a leg but it's him nonetheless."

A loud gasp rumbled through the growing crowd of onlookers at the mention of the name.

Luke turned in the saddle. "You can put 'im alongside his brother if you have a mind to. And you can mark 'em both as cold-blooded killers, 'cause that's exactly what they were—both of 'em—nothing but back-shootin' cold-blooded killers."

Luke nudged Mousy along the street and when he drew up at the picket fence a man wearing a white coat was standing there. He had apparently heard all the commotion and walked out to see what was going on. The man smiled and gave a nod, then looking up the street, he pointed and asked, "Who's that yonder draped over the horse?"

"No need worrying 'bout him doc. He's beyond your help. But I'm hoping you can do something for this fine man here."

"What happened?"

"Injun got 'im . . . stuck a knife in 'im four nights back. I sewed 'im up as best I could but he broke loose and started bleeding on the inside."

"Let's get 'im on into the office so I can have a look."

With Luke taking Elam's shoulders and the doctor at his feet they moved him up the steps and through the door, laying him on a long table covered with a white cloth.

"This man's a friend of yours?" the doctor asked.

"Yes, he is. His name is Elam Langtry."

"Elam Langtry, the army scout?"

"Yes, sir, that's who he is alright. You know 'im?"

"No," the doctor answered honestly, "but I've heard of 'im as all men in the military have. I was stationed up at Fort Collins for a time; I was the fort doctor up there for four years."

Suddenly a door leading into another room opened and a tall, slender woman walked in carrying a pail of hot water.

"Just set it over there on the counter," the doctor said pointing.

The lady did as she was told then turned back to face Luke.

"Hon, this is . . . I'm sorry I didn't get your name."

"The name's Ludd, Luke Ludd. I'm the sheriff of Rising Star."

"Paul Fillmore is my name," the doctor said putting out his hand, "and that there is my lovely and very smart wife Dorothy."

Luke took the man's hand, "Glad to meet you doctor," then tipping his hat to the lady he said, "And you too, ma'am."

She nodded and gave a smile, "Glad to meet you, Sheriff Ludd."

"Yes, sir," the doctor broke in, "he's bleeding on the inside alright and he's lost a lot of blood. We're going to have to go in and see if we can patch 'im up."

While his wife prepared the wound the doctor worked at arranging tools on a silver tray and when he was finished he turned with a scalpel in his hand. "You may want to step back, Ludd. This might get messy."

"Ain't you going to give him something to kill the pain?" Luke asked.

"No need now. But if he wakes up I will. He's so close to being dead, if I give it to 'im now it might finish the job." With that said the doctor moved in. He cut and dug and as he did, his wife was doing her best to mop up what was running out.

"Is there anything I can do to help?" Luke asked.

The doctor jerked his head in the direction of the door, "You can go across to the Trail's End and have a drink, and I'll come and let you know when we're finished. But before you go, Mr. Ludd I'd like to take a look at that eye."

Luke pushed his hat back, "An arrow ricocheted off a rock, and the shaft came around and slapped me right in it. Thought for sure I was going to lose it."

The doctor crossed to the counter and when he turned back he had a small bottle in one hand and a little odd-shaped, stemmed glass in the other. "Here," he said, "put two drops of this here wash in the glass and fill it to the top with water, then put it over your eye, tilt your head back, and blink a half dozen or so times. Your eye will hopefully start feeling better in a couple of days."

Luke took what was offered. "It already feels some better," he said. "But I don't reckon a little more doctorin' would hurt anything." Then giving a thankful nod he added, "I'm obliged, Doc." Turning for the door he said. "On my way to the saloon I reckon I better ease by the jail and have a talk with Sheriff Padgett. I don't know why he ain't already been over here. I know he had to see me ride in with the body."

"Sheriff ain't in town," the doctor said. "Left out a week or so ago on the trail of some killers, three brothers by the name of Logan, they shot and killed the bartender down at the Sagebrush Saloon—shot 'im down in cold . . ." The doctor suddenly fell silent then, throwing a hand up toward the street he asked. "You're the man that killed Leonard Logan, aren't you? And that's Pots that you brought in over the saddle?"

Luke gave a nod, "Yes, sir, I'm the one that did the shootin' and you're right again, Doc, about that being Pots wrapped up in the bedroll."

The doctor shrugged his shoulders, "They killed old Charlie, two of 'em did anyway. I don't think the youngest one took a hand in it; he's a coward through and through, that Billy is. He's afraid of his own shadow. Or at least nobody seen 'im do any shootin'. But you can bet he's running with 'em. Just walked right in, Sid and Kirk did, and shot 'im down. He never stood a chance.

"They told old Barney—that's Barney Lancaster, he's the town drunk, and the one who empties the spittoons and cleans up around the saloon at night—that they killed 'im because he didn't do enough to stop you from killing Leonard." The doctor shook his head knowingly then added. "But they'll be in a mighty big heap of trouble if old Carl catches up with 'em. Yes, sir, you can count on that, you sure can, 'cause he's had enough of those Logans. Those boys have been running 'im ragged ever since their old paw drug out."

"Did he go after 'em by himself?"

"When he rode out he took a posse, but three days later they came back saying the Logan's were headed west for the badlands. They didn't figure they'd catch up with 'em so they turned back. But old Carl didn't come back with 'em. No sir and he won't come back either until the job's done. He'll either bring 'em back or die trying."

Luke motioned toward Elam with a hand, "You'll let me know won't you, Doc?"

"Yes, sir, Mr. Ludd, just as soon as he dies or I'm finished. Either way I'll be sure to let you know."

"I'd prefer it to be the latter."

"That's what we're all hoping for, Mr. Ludd, but sometimes as hard as we try, it just don't work out the way we want."

Luke gave an understanding nod, for he knew all too well that things did not always go as planned. If they did Elam would not be lying on that table with a hole in his side.

Out on the boardwalk Luke paused, looking along the street. For the most part the boardwalks were now empty except in front of the undertaker's office where a great many people had gathered, talking and laughing.

Luke rubbed his beard and thought about a shave and a good, long, hot bath, but first he needed to take care of the horses and the stabbing pain in his belly told him he needed to find something to eat.

Tailing the reins and with the travois rumbling along behind the dun, Luke started down the street in the direction of the livery stable. At the undertaker's he drew up and after tying the horses to the hitch rail he started up the steps. As he made his way the crowd of onlook-ers parted giving him free access to the door. Behind him voices whispered and somewhere among the crowd a young girl giggled.

Luke entered and was immediately met by a tall, skinny, hatchet-faced man with a hooked nose and a long dropping mustache. "The name's Proctor, Earl Proctor," the man said putting out his hand "And your name is?"

"Luke Ludd, I'm the feller who brought Pots Logan in. I was needin' to find out how much it's going to cost to put 'im in the ground, probably somewhere there near his brother if that's possible."

"Twenty dollars is my normal fee. And if I do say so myself we do an outstanding job here. Of course we can't do much with him because of his condition, but we'll put his remains in a nice box."

"I'm sure you do," Luke said then after a little time to think he added. "He didn't have but five dollars in his pockets when I shot 'im but he does have a fairly nice horse and saddle. I reckon it's down at the livery al-ready 'cause I didn't see 'im out front anywhere."

"Yes, I told a couple of the men to take the horse on and put him away . . . and you said something about five dollars."

Luke drew the money from his pocket and handed it over, then turned and started for the door.

"I know you'll be happy with our services, Mr. Ludd."

Luke did not reply with words, but slowly shook his head, and as he walked back out onto the boardwalk he noticed two young boys standing by the steps. "You boys want a job? I'll pay you a dime each."

The taller of the two looked up, "Doing what mister?"

"I want these horses rubbed down and rubbed down good."

"Yeah, we'll do it, but you'll have to give us the money first."

"That sounds like a fair deal to me," Luke said then reaching into his pocket he gave the boys the money. He led the horses on to the livery where he put each of them in a stall and gave them an extra scoop of grain; and after filling their troughs with water he pitched them down hay. He picked up his saddlebags and started out, but he stopped at the door and looked back to see the two boys were working hard at earning their money.

At the café, Luke dropped into a chair at a little table just inside the door. There was a window where he could look out and see along the street from one end to the other. The crowd that had been in front of the undertaker's had gone and the clatter of footsteps could be heard coming and going along the boardwalk. Sweetwater seemed to be a peaceful little town with few people and even fewer cares. But a person did not have to be in town long before learning that Sweetwater's biggest problem was the Logans. Now there were two known dead and the other three were on the run. From the way Paul Fillmore had talked they might be dead too, if Carl Padgett had anything to do with it.

"What will it be, mister?" a voice asked.

Luke looked up to see an older lady with thinning

gray hair. "Have you got any stew and maybe a piece or two of cornbread?"

"Stew and cornbread coming right up," she said turning back for the kitchen.

"And I'll have some coffee too," Luke called out after her.

It was not long before he was eating some of the best stew he had ever tasted. He was finishing his fourth cup of coffee when he saw the doctor coming across the street. As he entered, Luke waved him over. "How's he doing?" he asked as the doctor took a seat.

"It's hard to say right now but at least he's alive . . . and resting. And if he lives through the night, then we'll know more tomorrow."

"I sure do want to thank you for patchin' 'im up doc."

"No, I should be thanking you."

"Why's that?" Luke questioned.

"You saved your friend's life; if you hadn't sewed him up he would have bled out. There's no doubt in mind . . . he would never have made it to town."

Luke smiled at the thought that he might have done some good, and he thanked his lucky stars that he did not go ahead and lance the knot when Elam had wanted him to. "Turnabout is fair play," Luke said. "That old man over in your office has saved my bacon more than once in the past. I wouldn't be here today or nowhere else for that matter if not for him and his brother."

The doctor stood. "You can see 'im whenever you want, but I gave him a double dose of laudanum. I doubt if he'd know you're there until late tomorrow or maybe even the next day. If I was you I'd go get some rest. It looks to me like it's been a while since you've had any sleep."

"It's been a rightly spell," Luke admitted, then taking the doctor's hand he said, "Keep track of what I owe and I'll make sure you get paid before I ride out."

At the hotel, Luke got a room and ordered a bath and while the tub was being filled, he shaved. Then he shook out of his clothes and slipped into the hot water. Twice he dozed off, once awakening only after his head went completely under and he came up fighting for air. Realizing how dangerous it was to bathe and sleep at the same time he dried off and stretched out across the bed.

The next time he opened his eyes the room was dark, and somewhere in the distance a piano was being played. He lay for a long moment considering the situation, then stumbled across to the window and drew back the curtain.

The lanterns along the street were lit and light shined bright from the windows of the Trail's End Saloon across the street. It was from there that the music was coming.

Luke crossed to the table and lighted the lamp then dropped down to the side of the bed. Slowly he tested his injured eye with a finger, and finding it not as tender to the touch as it had been, he rubbed to clear away the watery crust. He ran his fingers briskly through his tangled head of hair. Finally he stretched his arms high above his head and flexed his back, first one way then another and as he did he gave a long, howling yawn. Then dropping his head deep into his hands he sat for a long moment.

He needed coffee and needed it badly but first he would have to put on some clothes. When he had, he combed his hair and stomped into his boots. Swinging his gun belt around his hips he buckled it in place. Noticing the little glass he remembered what the doctor had said and following the instructions he doctored his eye and even though it burned a little it immediately felt better. He stopped at the door, took his hat from the peg, and after giving it a good hard dusting against his leg he slapped it in place as he walked out into the dimly lit hall.

Luke made his way along the deserted boardwalk to the cafe, walked in, and took a seat at the very same little table he had been at earlier. Near the back an older man sat spooning a plate of food and at the next table a middle-aged man and woman ate with a little girl.

"What will it be?" a voice asked.

Luke looked up to see the same older lady with thinning, gray hair. "I'll have a cup of your finest coffee please, Ma'am, and if you want a cup, I'm buying."

The words brought a smile to the woman's tired, aged face and her eyes lit up, "Why thank you, sir," she said, "but I've already had my fill and if I drink coffee this late at night I can't seem to sleep. But I do thank you again for the offer." She turned for the kitchen and came back with a hot cup of steaming coffee in one hand and a plate of what appeared to be a big slice of pie in the other. "Here," she said as she put them down, "you look as if you could use some good apple pie."

"Much obliged," Luke said. "Now that does look awfully good."

"The best part is," she said as she turned back for the kitchen, "It's on the house."

"No need in that," Luke called after her. "I've got money."

"No, sir, I won't hear of it. It's the last piece and we're fixin' to close here in a bit. There's no need in letting it set overnight and dry out. No, sir, you go on and eat it. That's good pie and there's no need in letting it go to waste."

Luke smiled and gave a nod, then picking up the fork he began to eat. He had taken only the first bite when he realized the woman was telling the truth, the pie was good, awful good. As a matter of fact he thought it might be the best apple pie he had ever tasted. Even Mrs. Bitters, who cooked up a fine apple pie, would find herself climbing a tough hill to top this one.

With the pie gone Luke sat sipping coffee, and had just started his second cup when the door opened and he looked up to see an older man walk in. As he entered, the family that had been eating earlier said their good-byes and went out.

The man stood just inside the door and looked first one way, then the other. Noticing Luke he started in his direction.

He was a small man with a narrow body and skinny arms and he wore clothes that were long overdue for a washing. He had small round eyes that sat deep above high cheekbones and when he walked up his smile revealed a full mouth of rotten buck teeth.

"You the one that killed them two brothers, Pots and Leonard Logan?"

"Maybe," Luke replied. "Who's asking?"

The little man nervously mopped his hands on the front of his shirt, then putting out his right he said, "Lancaster is my name, Barney Lancaster. I work up the street at the Sagebrush. I know them fellows, known all five of 'em for as long as I can remember."

Luke took the man's hand, "Glad to meet you, Barney," then gesturing toward a chair he said, "Why don't you have a seat."

"I was there the night they shot 'im," he said as he dropped down, "the night they killed old Charlie, I was right there and seen 'em do it. That sorry Sid just walked through the door and shot 'im without saying a word. Then Kirk shot 'im at least two more times, maybe three."

"How 'bout the youngest one, Billy I think is his name. Was he there?"

The little man shook his head, "No, he wasn't around when the shootin' started, but he had been. Him and both his brothers had been in the saloon all day and were spurring Charlie purty hard 'bout one thing or another . . . mostly 'bout you gunnin' down Leonard. I knew it was leading to no good 'cause the longer it went on the madder them Logan boys got. By the time Charlie run 'em out of the place they were all three so drunk they could hardly stand up. Sid and Kirk came back a short time later and that's when it happened. They just walked right in and killed 'im. Old Charlie never had a chance."

"Do you know where they were headed when they rode out?"

Again the little man shook his head, "Maybe to Lub-

bock; they've got an uncle and two cousins living there.
Lord, I hope they don't hook up with those two. Them
two boys are worse than these ever thought 'bout bein',
especially that Toby." Then gesturing toward the empty
plate he asked, "Was that some of Mrs. Clara's fine apple pie?"

Luke nodded, "Yes sir it was, and let me tell you it
was mighty fine, some of the best I've ever eaten."

"I know," Barney said with a smile. "If I had ten
cents I'd get me a slice."

"No you wouldn't," Luke said.

The little man looked over surprised, and after giving what Luke had said some thought, he asked, "Why
not? It's a free country, ain't it?"

"You're right, Barney, this is a free country, but
whether this country is free or not don't have anything
to do with that being the last piece of apple pie. That
was the last one . . . there ain't no more."

"Barney," the lady called out from the kitchen, "why
in the world are you bothering that man? I told you,
Barney Lancaster, if you come in here not to bother the
folks and I better not hear you ask anyone for money."

"I'm not bothering anybody and I ain't askin' nobody for money. Me and the Sheriff's just sittin' here
having a friendly talk. Now if you're not too busy, Mrs.
Clara, I'd like to have a cup of coffee."

The lady filled a cup and as she set it down on the
table in front of the little man, Luke pushed to his feet.
"It's been good talkin' to you, Barney," he said, "but I
reckon I'd better be gettin' along."

"I ain't through talkin' yet," Barney replied, "and it

may be in your best interest to listen to what I've got to say."

"What can you tell me that I might want to hear?"

"They're comin' after you."

"Who's comin' after me?" Luke asked as he slowly dropped back into the chair.

"Sid and Kirk, they killed Padgett down by Willow Flats two days back. I seen Billy at the livery stable not more than two hours ago. He wanted some whisky, so I went to the Sagebrush and got 'im four bottles and took 'em back. That's when he told me that Kirk shot Padgett. They know 'bout you killing Pots too. He took the whisky and rode out. The last thing he said was they were coming back to kill you."

"If that's what they want to do then they know where to find me," Luke said. Getting back to his feet he reached into his pocket and took out some money and pitched it down on the table. "I'll buy your coffee," he said, "and there's enough there for you to have a little something to eat if you're hungry. If not, it's yours to do as you'd like."

"Why thank you, Sheriff. Thank you very much. And if I see them fellers I'll be sure to come let you know."

"You do that, Barney," Luke said as he stepped slowly toward the door, but before walking out he turned back and said, "you do that."

Out on the boardwalk Luke drew up and stood looking along the street. If Barney was to be believed, Sheriff Padgett was dead. Killed by Kirk Logan and the Logans, who were fully aware that Luke had killed two of their brothers and that he was in town. Slowly he reached down and slipped the leather thong from the hammer of his Colt and loosened it in the holster. Then he turned and started along the boardwalk in the direction of the doctor's office. He stayed well to the shadows for he knew that just because Billy had said they would be back did not mean they were not already in town and if they were, Luke did not see any reason to make it easy for them.

At the door, Luke knocked and the lady answered. "Thought I'd come by and check on Elam."

The lady took a short step back to let Luke enter. "Come right on in," she said, "but I think he's still sleeping."

"I'm not going to bother 'im, ma'am," and realizing he was still wearing his hat in the presence of a lady he reached up and snatched it from his head, then said, "just thought I might look in on 'im. You know he'd be madder than all get out if he knew I didn't." Luke flashed a playful grin. "Who knows what that old rascal might say. He'd probably go telling his niece some sort of foolishness, like I left 'im to die by himself."

"Well in that case," the lady replied with a beautiful, wide smile. "I'd say to save your own hide you better look in on him." She turned and led the way down a hall to the third door, "He's right in there," she said as she nudged the door open. "And Sheriff, you're welcome to stay as long as you'd like."

"Much obliged, but I won't be long." After entering the dimly lit room, Luke crossed to the side of the bed and stood looking down into the drawn face of his friend. "I sure hate that I got you into this mess," he said in a whisper. Then reaching down he felt Elam's forehead and found it somewhat cooler to the touch than the last time he had checked; and his breathing was shallow but steady. All of a sudden the flame of the lamp by the bed flickered and at the window the curtains waved slightly as a cool breeze eased through. Luke reached for the cover to pull them up and when he did Elam's eyes opened.

"What are you doing?" he asked in nothing more than a faint, raspy whisper.

"Just pulling these covers up a mite so you won't get a chill," Luke answered surprised. Then he gestured toward the window, "Got a nice little westerly breeze coming in."

"Did you get the body delivered to the Sheriff?"

"Sheriff ain't here and I was told tonight by some drunk that he's probably dead. He said the Logans killed 'im out at a place called Willow Flats. You heard of it?"

"Carl's dead?" A voiced said from behind.

Luke spun at the unexpected voice and found it was the doctor who was doing the asking. "That's what I heard, but I heard it from that Barney Lancaster fellow. Say, Doc. Do you know where a place called Willow Flats is located?"

"Sure do. Used to be a trading post down east-southeast of here about fifteen miles. Just a big canvas tent was all it ever was, nothing fancy. But it kept the buffalo hunters supplied with cartridges, black powder and whisky. Heard tell that from time to time someone would trade the old man an Indian squaw or two and he'd have 'em there for his customers, but I don't know any of that to be true. But there's nothing there any more. The Indians raided the place one night, killed the old man, and burnt the tent to the ground." After a short pause he asked, "Why?"

"Oh, no reason really," Luke answered. "I just heard the name and thought I'd see if I could maybe find out where it's located."

"Is that where they killed Carl?"

Luke nodded his head, "I don't know for sure but that's what Barney told me, and he said he heard it from Billy Logan. Barney said that Billy told him that Kirk shot Padgett dead out at Willow Flats two days ago."

"Ain't the killing ever going to stop?" the Doc asked while shaking his head. "Now that they've killed Carl Padgett, who's next?"

"Maybe me," Luke answered, "Barney said they were coming after me." Luke paused and glanced down at Elam to find he had drifted off. "But anyway I better be gettin' along." At the door Luke looked back and said, "Doc, you'll be sure to let me know if anything changes here?"

"I sure will," was the answer.

Luke made his way from the doctor's office along the boardwalk to the hotel and in his room he crawled into bed. But as hard as he tried he could not get to sleep. He kept thinking about what Barney Lancaster had said—about his seeing two of the Logan brothers kill the bartender. And if that were not bad enough, Billy Logan had admitted to Barney that his brother Kirk had also shot and killed Carl Padgett.

Unable to sleep, Luke was up when the general store swung open its doors and after gathering a few supplies he saddled Mousy. Then, thinking he would probably be bringing back a body if he could find one, he saddled an extra horse. With that he mounted and rode from the livery heading east along the street; at the edge of town he swung east-southeast in the direction of Willow Flats.

Chapter Seven

The morning was quiet and the air cool when Luke started from Sweetwater. He rode along a deep, wide trail that over the years had been well traveled. He rode at a canter knowing that Willow Flats was a good fifteen miles away and if he was going to get there and back by morning he had a long, hard ride ahead. He was alert to the things around him and rode with great caution, one eye cast toward the ground looking for signs and the other on the distant horizon. He was well aware that the Logan brothers could be almost anywhere and they had already killed three innocent people, maybe four if Barney Lancaster was telling the truth and Carl Padgett was indeed dead.

The land that stretched before him was rough and broken, covered mostly by endless patches of mesquite, prickly pear, and prairie grass that stood tall. Long grassy spines covered with early morning dew glim-

139

mered in the dim sunlight as though each drop was a
sparkling diamond. The grass swayed back and fourth
in a light breeze, creating what appeared to be a sea of
shining waves as far as the eye could see. A more beautiful and peaceful sight Luke had never seen, and he
rode on taking in all the early morning beauty.

Here and there massive old oaks grew from the sides
of slopes and rocky ledges, and cottonwoods shot skyward along dry creek beds, and among them grew scrub
cedar. It was a hard, dry land that not long ago had held
great herds of buffalo providing much-needed food,
shelter and clothes for the Indians. It was land the Indians had at one time considered their own and at whose
hands no white man caught wandering through could
expect any measure of mercy.

A loud squelch drew Luke's attention and he looked
up just as a red-tailed hawk started its long dive from the
big white clouds. Luke reined in his horse to watch the
death-defying act and moments later the hawk swooped
in with his powerful talons extended and now sat with
his wings spread wide over its prey. "That's how fast it
can happen," Luke mumbled to himself. Then nudging
Mousy with a spur he worked his way south.

Mid-morning Luke drew within the shade of an oak,
its limbs hung low and twisted. After pulling the cork
from his canteen he drank his fill and sat looking over
the country while slowly wiping at his mouth with a
sleeve. Shoving the cork down tight he hung the canteen back over the pommel.

He sat studying the lay of the land with a careful eye.
He moved his line of sight quickly from one rock to an-

other and from one bush to the next and when he was satisfied that all was well on the ground, he turned his eyes toward the sky. He knew that if Padgett or anyone else was dead, the sky would be filled with buzzards. But after a long, careful search, not seeing as much as a single black-winged bird, he rode from the shade and worked his way south through a wide, almost impassable barrier of mesquite, thorns digging at his chaps and saddle leather as he moved among them.

Maybe, he thought as he rode, *just maybe, Kirk Logan has not killed Sheriff Padgett as Barney said. Maybe the whole story was just some scheme that Barney and the Logans had made up to get Luke away from town so they could take their revenge for his killing Pots and Leonard.* They might have guessed that if Luke was told the sheriff had been shot he would go looking for him and ride into an ambush.

By the time Luke stopped again the grass had lost its glimmer, the morning dew was now gone, sucked away by the hot sun, and the giant ball of yellow-orange fire hung high in the midday sky. Heat waves danced across the land distorting the shapes of all that lay beyond.

Luke quickly scanned the broken land, then looking skyward again searched the clouds. He spotted what he was looking for along the southern horizon, and the sight of the buzzards sent a cold chill up his spine.

Two hours further along the trail Luke spurred Mousy to the top of a small rise below which, stretching away into the distance, lay the glaring white expanse of the *playa* known as Willow Flats. Luke knew that even though it was dry now, during the rainy season the vast plain became a shallow lake and held water sometimes for weeks at a time. But now it was dry, and from the looks of the thick layer of crust and patches of scattered bunch grass it had been for quite some time.

Beyond the *playa* grew a thick line of willow and among them a sprinkling of salt cedar that stood tall against the distant blue sky. It was there that the buzzards circled, some riding the wind up high among the clouds and others sweeping low.

Luke rode off the rise, but it was not until he cleared the line of trees that he saw buzzards on the ground. As he approached, the ugly, red-headed, black scavengers squawked and took wing revealing the half-eaten carcass of a horse still wearing its saddle.

Not far away two coyotes stood from their resting place under a sagebrush and after giving Luke a quick look took off in a fast trot to the south. One stopped suddenly for just a brief moment and looked back in Luke's direction, but then turned in behind the leader.

Luke felt Mousy grow tense under him as they approached the dead horse. His ears perked and his legs stiffened and he snorted at the dreadful smell of death.

The extra horse, also knowing he did not like the smell, lowered his head and snorted, then quickly shied away, ripping the lead rope from Luke's hand. He went only as far as the tree line where he stopped and dropped his head.

Luke stepped from the saddle and tailing the reins he walked to where the dead horse lay. He figured this was Carl Padgett's horse but found no evidence that would make a positive identification. There was no sign of a brand because most of the flesh had already been eaten away and as near as Luke could tell there were no markings on the saddle other than what seemed to be a large, jagged hole in the left stirrup leather, and he knew the buzzards in their eating frenzy could have made that too. Furthermore, on the off-side the rifle boot hung empty and there was no canteen. It was evident by the advanced state of decay that the horse had been dead three or four days which would coincide with the story that Barney Lancaster had told.

Luke let his eyes search the terrain near and far but the body of Carl Padgett was nowhere to be seen and no other buzzards were near the ground. Dropping his eyes downward he began looking for signs as he walked in a tight circle around the dead horse. He made each pass a little wider until he was clear of the ground the animals and birds had disturbed, and it was in this undisturbed area that he found his first clue. It was just half a footprint but enough that Luke could tell it had been left behind by the heel of a boot. Just a few feet away he saw a dark spot on the ground that he figured to be blood, but it was not until he dabbed his finger in it and took it up to his nose that he knew his hunch was right.

He walked until he came to a spot where someone had apparently fallen. A large area of blood had soaked into the earth where whoever it was had laid and bled a good while. The sand was loosened where he had struggled to get back to his feet, and there was a deep indention where the butt of a rifle had been put down in the sand. Luke stood looking west in the direction of the trail but still he saw nothing of Carl Padgett, and off in that direction there were no buzzards flying about.

Stepping into leather Luke rode back for the extra horse, then started west. As he made his way he wondered why, if it was Carl leaving the trail, he was going west and not north toward Sweetwater. Luke knew that an injured man might do something he would not normally do and not realize he was doing it, like walk west when he thought for sure he was headed north.

Luke followed the trail west for the better part of an hour, having to swing down from the saddle in two places for a closer look at where whoever it was had again fallen and bled, stumbling back to his feet each time he had moved on.

Suddenly, Luke caught a slight glimpse of a distant reflection and immediately dove from his horse. Landing head first on the ground, he lay still for a long moment expecting to hear a gunshot, but when that did not happen he slowly got to his knees, and stretched only enough to see over the top of the tall grass. Slowly he looked over the area where he thought he had seen the reflection. But the search revealed nothing and the reflection came no more. Luke slowly stood keeping his eyes focused in that direction but again he saw nothing.

After giving the situation much consideration he slowly gathered the reins and crawled into the saddle but had no more than gotten himself upright when he saw the reflection again. Not knowing what it was, but figuring it was not a gun or he would already have heard a shot, he gave Mousy his head and rode toward it. Only when he rode to within clear view and saw it was nothing more than a canteen did he relax his finger on the trigger of his Winchester and let the rifle drop back to its resting place over the pommel. He realized that what had made it seem more than it was was the fact that it was caught about halfway up a low mesquite making it about the same height as a man on his knees holding a rifle.

Luke stretched tall in the stirrups and looked west in the direction of a small stand of tall cottonwood no more than two hundred yards away and figured that he would find the body in among those trees. He rode on and after crossing a narrow, shallow wash, he worked his way around a patch of prickly pear. Then riding up on a wash that was much deeper and wider than the last, he slowly eased to the bottom. In that rocky bottom he noticed movement out of the corner of his eye. Luke quickly glanced right at a hat blowing among the rocks and he saw a body. His face stiffened when he realized it was Carl Padgett. He lay face down, his body twisted among the rocks. Luke could see clearly where the Sheriff had slid down the side to the bottom of the wash but there were no signs of where he had tried to go up. Apparently he had made it down but had not had enough strength left to crawl out or even attempt it.

Luke slid from the saddle and when he reached to turn over the body he heard a low moan. "Carl," Luke called. Taking the man's shoulder Luke turned him onto his back and his eyes opened wide. His face was tight and his lips dry and cracked.

Luke took the canteen from the pommel and, slowly raising Carl's head, put the spout to his lips. The wounded man drank hungrily of the cool water until Luke pulled it away. "You better slow down there a mite," Luke suggested. After a moment he put the canteen back to his lips and Carl drank again. "Can you talk?" Luke asked.

Carl tried to speak, and his mouth did a fair job at forming the words, but no sound came out.

"Who did this, Carl?" Luke questioned. "Was it the Logans?"

Again he tried hard to answer, but when he realized he could not, he faintly nodded his head, "Yes."

"Was it all three of 'em?"

Carl shook his head, then with a weak, shaky hand showed only two fingers.

"Sid and Kirk?" Luke asked.

Again Carl nodded his head. Then as clear as any man could speak he said, "Pots."

Even though "Pots" was the only word spoken, Luke had a good idea of what Carl was trying to say so he answered, "Yes, sir, I got 'im, but there's no need in us talking 'bout that now. What we need to do now is get you moved over to that little stand of cottonwood yonder so I can take a look at your leg." Luke took Carl by the hand but when he started pulling him up he let out a loud, painful grunt and Luke felt Carl's body go limp as consciousness slipped away.

Very carefully, Luke eased Carl's limp body over the saddle, then after quickly gathering Carl's hat and rifle he stepped into the saddle and they rode up out of the wash and made their way slowly and easily to the stand of cottonwood.

Luke wasted no time. Taking his bedroll from the saddle he shook it loose and spread it over a thick stand of bunch grass. Pulling Carl from the saddle he carried him in his arms and put him down on the bed.

Luke moved quickly among the trees gathering enough wood to start a fire, then filling the coffee pot and a small pan with water he set them over the flames. While the coffee cooked Luke stripped the gear from the horses, led them to a little grassy knoll, and put on the hobbles.

When the water was warm Luke began cleaning Carl's wound. He noticed what looked to be a piece of bandana stuck deep in the hole where the bullet had entered the leg and another where the bullet had come out. The leg was swollen from the knee all the way up to the hip, and it was bruised black with pinkish lines. Luke knew that could be the first sign of blood poisoning. If that indeed was what this was the leg would have to come off, either here or back in town at Doc Fillmore's office.

Being careful not to disturb the pieces of bandana Luke finished cleaning the wound as best he could and wrapped it tightly with cloth from his saddlebag. Carl had lost a lot of blood and Luke did not know if he would recover, but if there was good news other than his still being alive, it was that the bullet had gone all the way through the meaty part of his upper left leg and from what Luke could tell had missed the bones completely.

With the wound taken care of and Carl stretched out on the bedroll asleep, Luke squatted on his heels at the fire, filled a cup with the hot coffee, gave it a cooling blow, and took a sip. *How in the world did he ever sur-*

vive four days out here in that condition? Luke thought as he took another sip. He knew the coyotes must have found the trail of blood and no more than a mile and a half away the sky was thick with hungry buzzards. Yet for some unknown reason neither the coyotes nor the buzzards had moved in for the kill. Maybe they had not realized that Padgett was near death and defenseless. The only conclusion Luke could reach is that the animals had been feasting on the dead horse and with their bellies full and plenty of food left they had not taken the chance to attack Carl, knowing he still moved, breathed, and made sound.

From what little Carl had said before passing out, it had only been two of the Logan boys doing the shooting, Kirk and Sid, the same two wanted in the senseless murder of Charlie the bartender.

Luke finished the coffee, filled the cup again and walked to the edge of the trees. To the west a thick line of dark gray clouds was building and behind them the sun glowed brightly, its rays gleaming through the narrow gap between the bottom of the clouds and the horizon in a spectacular array of yellow, orange and red colors that streaked the western sky. Luke stood taking in all the beauty of the setting sun but he knew that in time the bright colors would disappear, the sun's glow would fade, and night would come.

He let his eyes move slowly over the land in search of anything that would give him a clue that someone might be watching, a light wisp of smoke or dust, the reflection of a belt buckle or rifle barrel. As his eyes searched, he thought, *Are the Logans still out there someplace waiting for me to show myself so they can revenge their brother's death? Or maybe thinking they have killed the sheriff, have they gone back to town with the idea of doing what they want, knowing there would be no one there to stop them?*

They had killed the bartender, and there was no doubt in Luke's mind they thought they had killed the sheriff too. They had to know as reasonable men would, that the law would never let them get away with what they had done "But they're not reasonable men," Luke said under his breath.

Walking back to the fire he sliced bacon into a skillet. Then, cutting the top from a can of beans, he poured them into another pan and placed both where they would heat. Luke checked on the horses and on his way back gathered another load of firewood.

When the food was ready he dipped it to a plate and with the plate in one hand and a cup of coffee in the other he started in Carl's direction. "You 'bout ready to eat something?" Luke asked as he dropped down to a knee.

Carl's body flinched at the sudden voice, then his eyes slowly opened and he looked up. When he realized it was Luke doing the asking a faint smile came to his lips. "Am I dead?" he whispered, " 'Cause if I am, I'm still hungrier than a she-wolf with a litter of pups."

"You're as much alive as I am," Luke answered. Then pulling Carl up almost to a sitting position, Luke slid the saddle behind him where he could lean back against it. "I've got a good hot cup of coffee here, some bacon and a plate of beans. If that won't get you back on your feet, nothin' will."

"Sounds good," Carl said. He took the cup, but his hand shook and the coffee splashed.

"You want some help with that?"

Carl shook off the offer, "I can manage," he answered, then took a spoon of beans to his mouth.

When the cup was empty, Luke filled it again. When he handed it back Carl looked up and asked, "How'd you find me?"

"Had me a little talk with Barney Lancaster, he told me that Billy Logan said you were dead and that Kirk had killed you."

Carl ran his tongue slowly over his top lip and replied, "Well, he's only half right. Kirk shot me alright; him and that sorry brother of his ambushed me. If it hadn't been for you coming along when you did he'd probably been right on both. But you did, and I ain't." After a pause he asked, "Did you get Pots?"

"Yes, sir, sure did."

Carl gave a nod, "You know, Luke, with Pots locked up they'll be looking to burst 'im out."

"He ain't locked up," Luke replied. "I gave 'im the same two choices I gave Leonard, put his hands up or die, and like his brother he chose the latter, so I hauled 'im on down the street to Earl Proctor's place."

"Can't say I'm sorry to hear 'bout Pots being dead. It was bound to happen sooner or later," Carl said. "Did that fellow find you, that Elam Langtry? He walked into my office a day or two after you drug out, said he was kin."

"That's my wife's uncle, and yes, he did find me. None too soon either, Injuns had me pinned down in among some rocks. He took a bad cut down low on his side but he's back in town at Doc Fillmore's now gettin' patched up."

Carl pointed at his leg, "The bullet went all the way through. It went all the way through my leg and killed my horse. I tore my bandana in half, then I took a stick and packed a piece down deep in each side. Hurt like all get out but it sealed her right up."

"I saw you did. And that for sure might be what saved your bacon Carl." Luke pushed up slowly to his feet. "We better try to get some rest, Sheriff, 'cause if you feel up to a little ride, we'll head back to Sweetwater in the morning."

"I'll feel up to it alright. I can't wait to get my hands on those two sorry—"

Luke gave a worrisome nod, "We'll take care of those two when it comes time. For now you'd better try to get some rest." Taking Carl by the hand Luke drew him forward and at the same instant slid the saddle out, then lowered him down to the bedroll.

After adding wood to the fire Luke sat sipping coffee as he watched the flames grow. He thought of the long ride back to Sweetwater and what, if anything, he might find when he got there. It could be that the Logans, knowing the law would be coming after them, had ridden out. But neither of the two Logan boys that

Luke had dealt with acted as if they had good sense and both had made the wrong choice when Luke had called their hands. It was as though death meant nothing to them and if that was the case, Luke figured he would have to deal with the others as he had dealt with Pots and Leonard.

Luke stirred the fire with a stick and a whirling column of sparks rose from the ashes displaying every color imaginable before drifting high to fade into the night. A whippoorwill called from the east, and high in the tree above an owl sounded a broken hoot.

The moon hung high in the cloudless eastern sky among millions of bright, flickering stars. The moon's soft glow lay upon the land, bringing peace to the darkness and more importantly some visibility to the night.

Again Luke checked Carl to find he was still sleeping. Taking his extra blanket and rifle, he crossed to a giant oak at the north edge of camp and ducked under its low hanging limbs. Beside the trunk he dropped crossed-legged to the ground.

From time to time the night would come alive with sporadic yapping as coyotes fought over and ate at the dead horse to the east. Every time they cried out, it seemed as if the old owl let go a loud series of broken hoots.

Luke's eyes drifted slowly over the camp first to where the horses grazed, then to where Carl Padgett lay asleep. With all as it should be he lowered the rifle to rest across his lap. Then draping the blanket around his shoulders, he pulled his hat down over his eyes and leaned back against the tree.

It was still dark when Luke's eyes shot open, and he sat without moving for a long moment trying to figure out what had so abruptly brought him from his slumber. After a quick search of the camp turned up nothing out of place, he took hold of a low limb and pulled himself to his feet. The old owl hooted his dissatisfaction at the sudden movement and took wing. Then a low, jerky moan came from where Carl was asleep, and Luke knew that it was probably the moaning that had awakened him.

Luke crossed to where the fire still smoldered and added a handful of dry leaves. Dropping to one knee he blew at the ashes until white smoke whirled up and the flames flickered as they struggled to come back to life. When they had, he added wood. After filling the coffee pot with water he sliced bacon into a skillet and while the food cooked Luke gathered the horses and led them back to camp.

"Is it morning already?"

Luke turned in the direction of the unexpected voice, and realizing it was Carl doing the talking he answered, "Near 'bout. How you feel?"

"I've got to admit I have felt better."

"Good enough to ride?" Luke asked.

"Yes, sir, I can ride, but I'm a mite thirsty right now. Got any water there in that canteen?"

"Bet there is," Luke answered. Then raising Carl to a sitting position, he uncorked the canteen and handed it over.

Carl took a long pull of the canteen and said, "That bacon smell's awfully good."

"It'll be ready here in a bit, and some coffee too." Then after taking a little time to think Luke added, "Carl if you don't feel up to riding this morning just say so 'cause we can rest up here for another day or two or longer if you need to. We don't have to go today."

"Oh, I'll be alright. The leg's hurtin' like all get out but it's going to be doing that no matter what, so I might as well be riding. From the looks of those pink streaks I'd say I might need to get on back to town so Doc Fillmore can have a look at it. You know yourself, Luke, there's nothing worse than a one-legged sheriff."

Luke's body shuddered at the statement. He had thought the same thing when he first saw it—about the pink lines being blood poisoning—but he didn't see any reason to say anything.

"Can you take it off?" Carl asked quietly. "If it is blood poisoning?"

A sudden cold stiffness settled over Luke's face. Looking at the man on the bedroll he nodded his head, "Yes, to save your life I will. But, Carl, we don't know for sure that's what it is. It might just be the color of the bruise."

"Maybe so," Carl replied. "But I've seen blood poisoning a time or two in my life and if that's what it is you'll have to take it off."

Luke gave a nod. Then trying to lighten the conversation he chuckled and said, "Carl, I've always said that a good one-legged sheriff is way better than a bad two-legged one."

Caught off guard, Carl let out a loud, roaring belly laugh, "Well, Luke, you might be right, I've never looked at it quite like that."

After the food was eaten and the coffee finished, Luke saddled the horses; it was time to see about getting Carl up in the saddle. He knew there would be pain, but hopefully not enough to cause Carl to pass out again.

Luke thought for a moment about letting Carl put his arm around his neck for support to hop on his one good leg, but that meant he would have to try standing on his bad leg while he put his other foot in the stirrup. Realizing there was but one way to get Carl in the saddle Luke turned and asked, "You ready?" Before Carl could answer Luke scooped him into his arms. Carl cried out as Luke eased him up over the saddle. His body shook with growing pain and his face turned pale, but somehow he held onto consciousness. Luke stood holding the horse while the pain settled and when it had he said, "Sorry, Carl but that was the only way."

Carl gasped for air as he bit hard at his lip. "That's what I was dreadin'," he groaned "but now it's over and done with."

Luke rolled up the bedroll and latched it in place behind Carl's saddle. He stepped into leather and after giving Carl a look and nod they started north.

He did not know how long Carl could bear the pain of being in the saddle, but he was sure that if they were not back in Sweetwater by dark he would have no choice but to take off his leg. At the same time he was also sure that after what Carl had been through he might not survive it.

It was mid-morning before Luke slowed up again. The sun shone hot from the eastern sky and the increasing heat was already showing on Carl. His face was pale and stiff, and sweat ran freely from his brow and had already soaked his shirt both front and back. He rode slumped in the saddle and for the most part unaware of his surroundings and unsure of where he was. When Luke spoke Carl did not acknowledge that he had heard, but he did drink from the canteen when it was offered.

In the shade of a tall cottonwood, Luke tried talking Carl down from the saddle so he could maybe rest and cool, but any attempt was met with an onslaught of hysterical mumbling and Carl deliberately securing himself to the saddle by grasping the pommel tight with both hands, obvious signs of delirium brought on by unrelenting pain and growing fever.

Knowing that things were only going to get worse as the day wore on, Luke stepped back into his saddle and continued north, now at a quickened pace. He knew it was only a matter of time before Carl would not be able to ride any further and that would mean making a travois to haul him the rest of the way to Sweetwater or making camp—and making a camp would mean cutting off his leg. To do that Luke would need water to clean the nub once he removed the leg and got it seared over, and the way Carl had been consuming water both canteens were almost dry.

It was a little past midday when Luke crossed a trail and he drew up to have a close look. There were two sets of horse tracks, both carrying riders, but the part that really caught his eye was the fact that the horses were wearing no iron on their feet, a sure sign of Indians. The good thing was they were traveling east to west and the tracks had been left two or three hours earlier.

"Indians," a voice mumbled.

Luke looked in Carl's direction and said, "Horses ain't shod so I'm a-figurin' it is." He waited for a response but when he got none he asked, "Carl, you want a sip of water?" Again he got no answer. Pulling the cork he put the canteen up to Carl's lips but the man showed no interest in the canteen or the water inside it. "Here," Luke said, "you need to drink something."

Carl grunted and at the same moment his head tilted back and his mouth fell open.

Luke stretched tall and filled Carl's mouth with a small amount of water and he gulped it down but when Luke filled his mouth again, Carl choked on the liquid and had to cough several times to clear his wind pipe. "What are you trying to do, kill me?" He asked in a whisper.

"Just trying to get some water in you," Luke answered. "Here try another little shot."

"Just hand me the canteen, Luke, and I'll get my own drink."

Luke handed it over and Carl drank. When he was finished he handed it back and said, "Now see how easy that was."

Luke smiled at Carl's simple and witty attitude and answered, "Yes, sir, I sure do." Then something drew his eyes skyward and he observed several buzzards circling. At that moment he realized the nature and seriousness of the situation and could find no humor in it, only death. He glanced at Carl who sat slumped in the saddle; his head hung low and his hands gripping the pommel hard. Luke got the awful feeling that he was looking at a dead man. Even though Carl was still breathing, he was probably dead; he just hadn't fallen from the horse yet. Luke knew too, that with each step they were getting a little closer to Sweetwater and to the doctor. He gathered the reins and swung up touching Mousy with an easy spur. He knew that his destination could be no more than five or six miles away.

They rode through the heat of late afternoon stopping from time to time to let Carl drink. To the east a dust devil grew from the ground, whipping at the thorny limbs of the mesquite as it whirled its way, and then, just as it had started, it ended with a whisper and faded back into the earth.

Suddenly Luke heard a loud groan followed by a thud and when he turned he saw Carl Padgett lying face down on the ground. Luke drew in hard on Mousy and slid down on the run. He quickly checked the side of Carl's neck for a pulse and a sigh of relief rolled from his lips when he found one. The beat was weak and Luke knew time was running out. It was evident that Carl could no longer open his eyes much less sit in a saddle.

Luke pushed up to his feet and quickly searched for anything big enough to make the side poles of a travois but unable to see anything but twisted mesquite he decided against it. He pulled Carl up and heaved him onto his shoulder and then carried him to the horses and slid him over the saddle. After tying him on, Luke stepped up and rode at a canter toward Sweetwater.

To the west the sun's bright orange glow hung near the horizon, and it was fading fast with each passing moment. The evening had started to cool and soon it would be dark; and if Luke stood any chance of saving Carl Padgett's life he must keep moving toward town where he would get the help he needed. Even then Luke did not know if it would be enough.

Luke's body ached from the long day in the saddle and hunger pains stabbed his insides, but he pushed those concerns aside and rode on working his way through the never-ending maze of mesquite. Then under the last glimmer of daylight Luke rode to the top of a rise just above the little town of Sweetwater. He looked back at Carl, and wanted to tell him they had made it but, knowing he would not hear, Luke simply nudged Mousy and rode down from the rise.

A short time later he drew up to the hitch rail in front of the doctor's office. Before he had time to swing down the door opened, and a big smile came to his face when he saw Paul and Dorothy Fillmore step out.

"Is he dead?" the doctor asked.

"No he ain't, or he wasn't the last time I checked. But he's in bad shape, Doc . . . almost got his leg blown off."

"Well, let's get 'im down and inside so I can have a look."

Carl let out a groan as Luke pulled him from the saddle. With the doctor taking Carl's feet they moved up the steps and through the door.

Without delay Paul Fillmore cut the pant leg but when he threw it back he froze. Then, turning, he slowly placed the knife back on the tray. Looking over at Luke he shook his head and said, "He may live—and I'm not going to say for sure he will. But I will say that if he does he'll just have one leg 'cause that thing is full of blood poisoning and should have been done away with at least two days ago."

"The poison was already in his leg when I found 'im," Luke answered. "We talked 'bout taking it off but I didn't have anything but my knife to do it with. I figured it would be better if I could get 'im in here to you."

"That was probably the right thing to do. The poison had already set in and if you had cut if off he probably would have bled to death." The doctor paused then looking at his wife he said, "We know what has to be done so we might as well get started."

"I'll heat some water," Dorothy Fillmore said as she started for the door.

"Can I be of any help?" Luke asked.

"Nothing you can do here," the doctor replied.

Luke gave a nod and started down the hall to check on Elam. When he opened the door a terrible feeling washed over him. The bed was empty—not only empty but freshly made. Luke spun on his heels and as he reentered the room where the doctor was he asked, "Where's Elam?"

"Gone."

"Gone," Luke echoed quietly. "But he was talking just before I left, and he had good color."

The doctor chuckled, "Not gone like dead. He's just gone. He said being cooped up inside was killing 'im so he left. He's down at the livery bedded down in one of the stalls. He ain't gettin' around too good, but he's doing alright, still a little sore—but he will be for several more days. You thought I meant he was dead?" the doctor asked with a laugh. "Lord, no. That old codger ain't dead. He's too mean to die. He wanted to come looking for you and the only thing that kept 'im from it was that he couldn't get his foot in the stirrup." The door opened and Mrs. Fillmore walked in carrying a pail of hot water. "Anyway," the doctor said, "that's where you'll find 'im."

Back at the hitch rail, Luke gathered the horses and started along the street in the direction of the livery stable. As he made his way his eyes were constantly moving, searching each window and dark alleyway for any sign of the Logans, for he had the uneasy feeling they were nearby and sooner or later would show their hand. Luke smiled at the thought, but right now he needed to check on Elam.

Chapter Eight

In front of the Trail's End Saloon, Luke left the horses tied to the rail. In anticipation of seeing one or all of the Logans inside he reached down and slipped the leather thong from over the hammer of his Colt, and as he made his way up the steps he loosened it in the holster.

Loud music came from the inside and a young woman could be heard singing. She seemed to be struggling to stay in tune with the piano as it played "Over the Sea." Luke pushed through the batwing doors to find the long, narrow room filled with men. Tobacco smoke hung heavy in the air, and off in one corner four men sat at a little table playing a game of cards, and half a dozen more stood along the bar. But all eyes turned to Luke when he entered and there was a sudden rush of sliding chairs when many of the men turned to get a better look.

Luke drew up just inside the door and stood while his eyes adjusted to the brighter light and then moved deeper into the room. He had not made it halfway to the bar when a short, thin woman approached him wearing a big, wide smile, "Hey, handsome," she started, "would you buy a lady a drink?"

"No, I wouldn't," Luke replied abruptly. "And furthermore you shouldn't be asking men you don't know any such question. They might get the idea that you're a loose woman."

Hearing the unexpectedly harsh words, the woman's smile quickly faded, and a frown took in its place. "Just trying to make a living," she said, then turned and draped her skinny arms around the neck of a drunken cowboy.

"What will it be, stranger?" the bartender asked as Luke leaned an elbow on the bar. Then noticing the star he straightened and said, "Sorry, Sheriff. What can I get you?"

"Give me a whisky," Luke answered, pitching down a dollar; it rang out when it hit the bar.

The bartender filled a glass with his finest whisky and as he pushed it across he pointed at the payment and said, "Your money's no good in here, no sir. And I expect you'll find it that way in most places in town. We're in your debt, Sheriff, for doing away with Pots and Leonard . . . nothing but troublemakers both 'em, and I can't say that I'm the least bit sorry they finally got what was due 'em."

Luke nodded a thank-you, then picking up the glass he tossed down the whisky. When he set the glass back on the bar it was filled again. "Have you seen 'em?" Luke asked.

"The Logans?"

"Yeah, Sid and Kirk . . . I need to talk to 'em."

"No I haven't. And they're not welcome in here and they know it. I ran 'em out back when I first opened this place. They moved their business on down the street to the Sagebrush." He wiped the bar with a rag. "I don't know who's going to look after that place now that Charlie's dead. That's a shame, them just walking in and shootin' 'im dead like they did. I heard just a bit ago that you hauled Carl Padgett in to the Doc's office. Is he going to be alright?"

Luke gave a long doubtful sigh. "Hard to say, but old saw-bones is over there now takin' his leg off. Bullet hole got a big dose of blood poisoning in it."

The bartender shook his head sadly at the news while wiping the inside of a whisky glass. "They did it—the Logans. I'd stake my life on it. They killed Charlie and I'll bet you a dollar they're the ones who shot Carl."

"That's sure the way it looks to me," Luke answered knowingly, "Or at least Carl told me they did it."

"Sure hate to hear that 'bout Carl, but I knew it was bound to happen sooner or later. You know, him and those boys ain't got along from day one. But on the other hand ain't nobody else got along with 'em either."

"You'll let me know if you see 'em," Luke asked, then tossing down the second drink he set the glass on the bar and waved off the refill, starting for the door.

"I sure will," the bartender said with a nod, "I sure will, Sheriff. You can count on that."

Luke threw up an easy good-bye hand when he got to

the door. Out on the boardwalk he stood letting his eyes search the street but still saw nothing of the Logans. Stepping down to the street he took up the reins and started toward the livery, but had taken only a few steps when he saw a dark shadow duck into the alleyway between the Sagebrush Saloon and Blackman's General Store. The shadow moved quickly, but Luke had seen enough to know it was a smaller man wearing a big-brimmed hat. Not knowing who it was or what he was up to, Luke pulled the horses up on either side of him.

No light could be seen through the dusty windows along the front of the Sagebrush Saloon, there were no horses tied at the hitch rail, and no one moved along the boardwalk. All the signs of a place as dead as the man who had run it until just a few days ago.

Why had the man wearing the big-brimmed hat so quickly ducked into the alley? Was he one of the Logans or was it Barney, the town drunk? Maybe it was just a well-meaning citizen taking a shortcut home. Luke did not know for sure, and he would not know Sid and Kirk Logan, or their brother Billy, if they walked up face-to-face with him. He had never laid eyes on any of them.

All Luke knew for sure was that the shadow had appeared to be that of a short, thin man like Barney. Luke remembered clearly that Barney had not been wearing a hat of any kind when they had talked. Whoever this was had not wanted Luke to see him duck into the alley and Luke had a gut feeling that he was still there somewhere, watching.

When Luke reached the livery stable both large doors in front were standing wide open. A tall, wide-shouldered man with a thick, red beard and full head of collar-length hair of the same color was down on one knee working on a wagon wheel. While he went about his work he softly whistled a tune that sounded Irish, but upon seeing Luke he quickly stood up and met him with a loud, "Evening, stranger."

"They need a good rubdown and extra grain," Luke said, hanging the reins over the hitch rail. "And see to it they have plenty of water."

The big man arched his tired back and then, wiping the sweat from his brow with a sleeve, he gave a nod. "Rubdown and extra grain," he repeated.

"Have you got a man staying in one of these stalls?"

"Yeah, he's back there. But you better not pester 'im mister 'cause that old rascal will snap your head off. Hell, he might even shoot you."

Luke laughed, then moved on toward the back, but made his way staying close to the wall and out of view of anyone watching from the alley. When he got to the stall where Elam was bedded down in a thick pile of hay he walked past it and out the back door.

Behind the livery it was dark and the farther Luke got from the glare of the lanterns the less he could see. He made his way along the fence to where the darkness gave way to the dim light of the street lamps. He stopped and looked along the boardwalk in front of the Sagebrush, but as before saw no one and no movement. Stepping to his left he got into a position where he had a clear view along the back of the buildings but it was dark and if someone was there, friend or foe, he could not have seen them.

In front of the livery stable the big man had started stripping gear from the backs of Luke's tired horses while continuing to whistle the same tune. After hanging the saddles on the fence he began rubbing down the horses.

Hearing a thump, Luke looked up the street to see an older man walking with a cane along the boardwalk in front of the cafe. Across the way two cowboys gave a loud holler as they stumbled from the door of the Trail's End. Luke recognized them as two of the four men who had been playing cards.

Turning to the Sagebrush Luke reached down and drew his pistol. As he thumbed the hammer back he started into the dark shadows behind the buildings. Though he figured he was out of sight to anyone watching from the front of the alley, he moved slowly, one foot at a time. There might be two men in the alley, one watching the street and another the back.

At the corner of the general store Luke stopped and held his breath, listening, but the only sounds were from the piano at the Trail's End, and the persistent whistling at the livery stable. He eased along the wall with his pistol leading the way. The further he moved from the street the darker it got, and Luke sometimes had to feel his way around piles of wagon wheels or farm equipment.

Coming to the alley again Luke pulled back his hat and eased his head slowly to see around the corner. Near the back the alley was dark but the glow of street lamps lit up the two rain barrels on either side of the entrance. There was movement behind the barrel nearest the general store. Luke stood straight and focused his eyes more closely and when he saw the big-brimmed hat bobbing he knew for sure that someone had been watching him. Now the questions were who they were, and why were they watching him?

Luke eased around the corner alongside the building. With each step he was getting closer to finding out who was so interested in what he was doing.

Suddenly a man called out loud from up the street. Luke's pulse quickened and he instantly froze in his tracks. Only moments passed before a woman answered back and a short time later the air was filled only with fading laughter. As Luke moved closer he noticed the hat rose above the barrel for only a moment or two, then dropped back down, and rose again. When he was within arm's length he reached out and lightly tapped the hat brim with his gun barrel. "If you want to go on living, friend, I wouldn't make any quick moves."

"Don't shoot . . . don't shoot," a voice cried from under the hat. Luke immediately recognized the voice of Barney Lancaster.

"Barney, what are you doing? Trying to get your fool-self killed?"

"No, please don't shoot. Nothing, I ain't doing nothing," Barney answered in a shaky voice, then after a short time to think he added. "I was fixin' to go to bed. Yeah, that's right . . . this is where I bed down . . . I was fixin' to get me some shut-eye, 'till you came along and pestered me."

"Get on your feet," Luke said through gritted teeth, "and walk on over to the jail. And I swear if you do anything stupid I'll shoot you."

"Why do you want to shoot me? I ain't done nothing."

"Just shut up and start walking."

At the jail Luke lighted the lamp and as the flame grew on the wick the inside slowly emerged from the darkness. "Barney, I'm going to give you one chance and one chance only to come clean, and if you don't I'm going to lock you up for taking part in the shootin' of Carl Padgett."

The little man's eyes suddenly grew, "I didn't shoot anybody I swear, Sheriff. I swear on my poor old mammy's grave. I didn't. And if anybody says I did they're wrong, they're just plain wrong . . .'cause I didn't shoot anybody. Sid and Kirk shot old Charlie . . . just walked right into the Sagebrush and shot 'im down. He was cleaning the bar, and Billy told me out of his own mouth that Kirk shot Carl." The little man wiped his long, narrow, dirty face with a shaky hand. "You were right, I was watching you from the alley, but Sid told me to, and he said that if I didn't let 'im know when you got back to town he would kill me. They're out there at the house now waitin' on word. They're going to kill you, Sheriff. They've killed Charlie and Carl and now they're going to kill you."

"I hate to be the one to tell 'em but Carl ain't dead. He's over at the Doc's right now gettin' patched up."

"Carl ain't dead," Barney echoed. "But . . . but Billy . . . but Billy said Kirk killed 'im—said he shot 'im dead out at Willow Flats."

"Oh, they shot 'im alright," Luke said. "And he might eventually die, but he ain't dead yet." After taking time to study the situation, he added, "Barney, you said they're out at the farm waitin' on word?"

"That's right, Sheriff. They said when I saw you to come let 'em know."

"Well that's exactly what I want you to do, Barney. I want you to go tell 'em that I'm back and I'm talking around town about how easy it was to kill Pots and Leonard . . . and you can tell 'em that I'm going to get a posse together at first light and come after 'em."

"Oh I see, Sheriff, you're a-thinking that you've maybe bitten off more than you can chew and you're wantin' 'em to run."

"No I can chew my part, but if they took off wouldn't that be better for everyone? This ain't my fight, Barney, and there's not a reason in the world that I should stick my nose in where it don't belong and take a chance of gettin' myself killed. I'm only one man and there's three of them."

"You could back-shoot 'em Sheriff. That's the way I'd do it . . . I'd catch 'em not looking and back-shoot ever' last one of 'em."

"I'm sure you would, Barney, but it would still be better yet if I didn't have to do anything. I'll be gone back to Rising Star in a day or two and with Carl laid up or maybe even dead they can come back and run the town to suit themselves. They could even make you the mayor of Sweetwater."

"No, I wouldn't want that job," Barney replied. "But you said yourself that Carl might not make it, and if he don't I wouldn't mind being the sheriff."

The words stung Luke's ears and the nonchalant way they were spoken made it even worse. Suddenly he found himself having to fight the urge to kill Barney

Lancaster, though Luke did not realize how close he had come until he looked down and noticed his hand resting on his pistol butt. Slowly he relaxed his hand and then forced a thin smile at Barney and said, "I don't know why they wouldn't let you be sheriff; I think you'd make a good 'un."

Barney showed his rotten teeth behind a proud smile and clapped his hands together. "Do you? Do you really think I'd make a good sheriff?"

Luke put his hand lightly on the man's shoulder, "I think you'd make a darn good sheriff, I really do, Barney. But you better get going because the sooner you get there the sooner they can light a shuck. You know as well as I do we need 'em to get a head start because if I lead the posse all the way out to the farm and they're still there, then I'll have no other choice but to arrest 'em."

"Okay, Sheriff." Crossing to the door Barney walked out with Luke following behind.

"Now remember to tell 'em exactly what I said about how easy it was for me to kill Pots and Leonard and that I said it's not my fight."

"Okay, Sheriff. I'll tell 'em exactly what you said."

Luke stood on the boardwalk and watched the skinny little man go, the big-brimmed hat flopping as he ran toward the livery. Luke knew the Logans would never run but he also knew that if they did he would hunt them down. His hope was that by sending Barney with word that he was back in town and bragging about killing their brothers, it would put a burr under their blankets, and they would come looking for him. Luke wanted them to come to town because then he would have a better chance of arresting them without gunplay. He also knew that if he went out to the farm they would have the advantage.

Luke heard hooves pounding and saw Barney coming at a dead run throwing up a hand as he passed. Luke watched until he was out of sight and then he turned back toward the livery.

Elam appeared to be asleep when Luke entered the stall but when he heard the unmistakable click of a hammer being thumbed back he asked, "Elam, you awake?"

"Yes, I'm awake. Who can sleep with all that dang whistling going on? It wouldn't be so bad if it wasn't the same thing over and over again."

Luke gave a chuckle, "How you feeling?"

"A mite better since I moved out of that doctor's office. They were killin' me, Luke . . . they were just outright killin' me. I don't see how anybody can stand being cooped up like that. And that woman . . . that woman wanted me to bathe some part of my body ever' day. If it wasn't my face it was my hands and once she even wanted me to scrub my feet. Heck, my skin got plum wrinkled."

Luke laughed. "Well, I swear," he said clapping his hands together. "I've never heard of any such."

Elam gave a nod, "It was pure torment . . . yeah, torment, that's what it was, plain and simple. 'Course they called it docterin'." Then a slight smile formed on his lips. "But I will have to say she's been regular about bringing the grub around." All of a sudden the whistling grew louder, and Elam aggravatingly raised his head up from the hay, "My word, why don't somebody shoot 'im so he'll stop all that damn noise?" Then glancing over at Luke he said, "He did stop it once but just long enough to tell me it was going to cost ten cents a day to bed down in here."

Neither spoke for a good bit, then Elam asked, "Did you find the sheriff?"

"Yeah, I found 'im. Found his dead horse first, then I found Carl laying face down in a wash with his left leg almost shot off. He's over at the Doc's now. He's going to loose his leg."

"Blood poisoning?" Elam questioned.

"Yeah, and bad too. He might not make it."

"That's a shame." Then after a moment, Elam asked, "Luke, what you going to do 'bout it?"

"The Logans did it, and they killed the bartender over at the Sagebrush too. There's not but one thing I can do, Elam, I'm going to put 'em in jail. That is, unless they want to give me some kick and if they do we'll put 'em alongside Pots and Leonard."

"They might be a handful by yourself."

"I can handle the likes of the Logans. I've dealt with men like them for years."

"You better not take 'em lightly, Luke. They're a sneaky low-down bunch. And it might not be just those three you're dealing with; you know they've got them kinfolk over in Lubbock. From what I hear the whole bunch is about the same."

Near the front the big man's voice rang out with a loud, "Good evenin' Mrs. Fillmore. How are you this fine day?"

"Just fine, Mr. Baker. And you?"

"Fair, I reckon. I've still got a mite of soreness in my shoulder but that salve the Doc gave me seems to be helping."

"That's good. Maybe it'll get better . . . well I better be getting along . . . Now you be sure to tell Mrs. Baker I said hello."

"Oh, I will."

"Don't let her come in here," Elam blunted.

"Why?" Luke questioned. "She's probably bringing something to eat."

"That might be, but she's also going to want me to bathe something."

Moments later Dorothy Fillmore appeared in the doorway of the stall carrying a basket in one hand and a small coffee pot in the other. "Good evening, Mr. Langtry." She said with a bright, beautiful smile. "Sorry I'm so late but I've been tied up over at the office. I'll bet you're about to starve." Then glancing over she gave a welcoming nod, "Sheriff Ludd, how nice it is to see you again."

Luke tipped his hat. "Likewise, Mrs. Fillmore," Then after a short pause he asked, "How's Carl doing?"

Her expression suddenly turned somber. "Not well, I'm afraid." Then reaching into the basket she took out a wet towel, asking, "Mr. Langtry do you think you can wash your face and hands or do you want me to do it?"

Elam looked hard at Luke and disgustedly shook his head. "Don't need to," he answered. "I've already done that two times since morning."

"Well, you're fixing to eat so you need to do it

again," she said with a pleasant little laugh. "I've got some stew here and cornbread and, who knows, if you wash your face and hands without giving me any trouble I might even find a cup here in the basket for some coffee."

Elam looked at Luke, his eyes pleading for help.

Thinking it best not to interfere, Luke smiled and gave his shoulders a light shrug. "That stew smells awful good," he said. Then he threw up a hand in the direction of the cafe. "I think I'll mosey on over and see if Mrs. Clara has any left."

"Luke," Elam called out. "Luke, don't go. Luke, don't leave me here with this woman . . . Luke . . . Luke."

"Now, now, Mr. Langtry, this won't hurt a bit," Luke heard Dorothy Fillmore say as he left the stall.

"Let go . . . let go," Elam snorted. "I'll do it myself."

Luke laughed at the fact that the old hard-nosed army scout had apparently met his match.

Before leaving the livery he checked on the horses and after pitching them down more hay he walked to the café. He stepped quickly along the empty boardwalk, staying well within the shadows. Barncy had said the Logans were out at the farm but that didn't mean they were and he did not want to get caught in an ambush. If they were out at the farm it would be nearly daybreak before they could get back to town. That would give him time to eat and get some rest.

Mrs. Clara met him with a smile and said, "Good evening," when he entered the cafe. Before he was settled good she had brought a big plate of stew and a hot cup of coffee. It was late and with no other customers the old lady dropped into a chair at Luke's table, then leaning on an elbow she said, "They said Carl's in bad shape."

"He may not make it," Luke answered.

She pushed her hair back. "You know, son, the Logans are going to come after you."

"I figure there's a good chance of that," Luke answered, spooning the stew. He took a sip of coffee and said, "Let 'em come."

Getting back to her feet the old woman smiled, giving Luke a thankful pat on the shoulder. "Kirk's the one you'll need to look out for. After Leonard and Pots he's the meanest and the fastest with his gun. And it don't matter to 'im which side he shoots at, front or back."

"I'll be sure to keep that in mind," Luke said, then asked, "You wouldn't have a slice of that fine apple pie would you, Mrs. Clara?"

"No, I sure don't," she answered politely. "Old man Meeks got the last piece a bit ago. You know that's all he comes in here for, coffee and apple pie. I can't remember him ever gettin' anything else, just a cup of coffee and a slice of my apple pie."

"I don't blame 'im," Luke replied, "they're both mighty fine by themselves and they're even better together."

After the stew was gone Luke finished his coffee and when he tried to pay, his money was flatly refused. His insistence drew a scornful frown and stern warning from the old lady. "Son, this is my place and I charge what I want, when I want, and I say you don't owe me."

Luke thanked her and after putting his money back in his pocket headed for the door. The night was cool when he walked out onto the boardwalk, and from across the way light shone brightly from the windows of the Trail's End and piano music could be heard. Along the street the lamps rocked slightly in the light westerly breeze and the flames flickered. In the distance the sign hanging above the hotel squeaked softly as it swayed back and forth, and the bright light in the windows of the doctor's office indicated Paul and Dorothy Fillmore were still getting about.

Luke looked up and down the street wondering which way the Logans would come. They might ride straight into town, or they might leave their horses somewhere and sneak in on foot. Either way he had to be ready. Luke knew they would be coming, and there was no doubt in his mind they would be coming to kill him.

Now he needed rest for he had not slept in four days. His muscles ached from too much time in the saddle and his eyes felt gravelly, more so in the eye that had been injured by the arrow.

He had a room at the hotel but it was upstairs and when the Logans came they could easily leave one outside watching the windows while the other two came up the stairs and would have him trapped.

No, he thought, if he rested it would have to be in a place the Logans would not expect him to be, and where he could get out fast if need be. The jail was empty but that's where Barney had last seen him and where they might look first. There was the loft of livery stable but again that would leave him high with no escape. His eyes moved along the street to the far end where a sign read *The Sagebrush Saloon.*

Hearing a slight noise behind him, Luke spun and in the same instant dropped his hand for his pistol butt, but he stopped his draw when he realized it was Mrs. Clara bolting the door. Reaching up she slid the curtains closed.

Luke hitched his pants and started in the direction of the Sagebrush. The town was quiet now and the boardwalks deserted. The windows at the Trail's End still beamed brightly, but the piano was silent. Atop the sign at the land office an owl hooted at the moving shadow, and the dark sky hummed with the fluttering wings of bats swooping low in search of mosquitoes.

Luke stopped at the livery stable just long enough to slide his Winchester from the boot and a box of cartridges from his saddlebag. When he got to the Sagebrush he paused and listened, but hearing nothing, pushed open the doors with a loud squeak. He did not light the lantern or even a match in fear that someone might see the flame. He wanted it to appear to anyone looking in from the outside that the place was deserted. He made his way to the little table in the back where Leonard Logan had been sitting just before he killed him. He slid back a chain and sat down and looked through the window. From his position he could see the entire street clearly, from one end to the other.

Luke slowly and quietly worked the action on his rifle, loaded the chamber, and laid it on the table next to the box of shells, the barrel pointed directly at the door. With everything set he pulled down his hat, leaned back and, as his tired muscles relaxed, he closed his eyes.

Luke was not sure what had awakened him but left his eyelids closed and for a long moment did not move. He heard nothing. Ever so slowly he opened his eyes and peeked from under his hat brim to find nothing but night changing into the haziness of early morning.

"Why ain't they here?" he asked himself in a low voice. Luke knew that if Barney had delivered the message as he had told him to, the Logans should have already arrived. He looked down the street, but suddenly heard a horse snort. He looked back toward the livery stable until the wall blocked his line of sight.

Luke slowly took his rifle from the table and had just started to stand when he heard the horse again, then the sound of hooves stomping on hard ground, and a moment later another snort. He realized the noise was coming from the alley just on the other side of the wall. Suddenly someone pushed at the back door but it banged against the latch. A voice whispered, "It's bolted."

Even though he could not see he had the feeling it was the Logans—at least two of them, maybe all three. Luke dropped back down to the chair and waited. When he heard footsteps on the boardwalk he knew they were coming in the front. He readied the rifle on his shoulder and moved his finger over the trigger. Two men walked into view but stopped short of the door.

"Why don't we just go on over to the jail and kill

'im?" a third man who had not yet come into view asked. But before anyone could answer, Barney Lancaster stepped around the two men and pushed through the batwing doors. When he saw Luke he spun back and dove for the boardwalk.

Luke jumped to his feet, but before he could pull the trigger, two pistols barked lead through the window, sending glass flying, Luke fell to the floor and rolled, then pushing up to his knees he pulled off a shot just as the second of the two men went out of sight.

"They ain't goin' to let me be nothing if I don't kill you!" a voice shouted.

Luke turned to see Barney laying flat on his belly, looking under the batwing doors with a pistol in his hand. "You don't want to do . . ." Luke started, but his words were cut short by the deafening roar. The bullet went wide but Luke's did not and Barney Lancaster never knew what hit him.

Luke looked over the batwing doors to see a horse and rider break from the alley. As he raised his rifle a bullet splintered the door near his head, forcing him to duck. The bullet had come from somewhere near the livery. Standing up straight he brought the Winchester to his shoulder again and just as the horse and rider drew even with the jail he pulled the trigger. There was a loud scream as the bullet hit, and throwing up his hands the man tumbled headfirst to the ground. But he still lived and struggled back to his feet, stumbling toward the boardwalk. Luke took careful aim on the man's chest and pulled the trigger again. This time the man did not get up because the shot was true. He was dead.

Luke searched the dim morning light in the direction the shot that hit the door had come from but he saw nothing. If the shooter was still in position and Luke stepped out the door he would be a dead man. He moved quickly to the back door, knowing that every passing minute gave the killers more time to escape.

Luke walked close to the backs of the buildings, staying close to the wall, until he reached the corner of the general store and stopped. The sun was just peeking over the eastern horizon, marking the start of a new day, but the town had not begun to stir and the street was empty.

From where Luke stood it was a good thirty yards or more to the livery all out in the open. He would have to go fast and run in a jagged line to avoid giving someone an easy shot. He leaned his rifle against the wall, drew his pistol, and thumbed the hammer back, then focused his eyes on the corral east of the stable. Taking a deep breath he let it out slowly and broke from the cover of the building in a dead run. To his surprise no shots rang out. He slowed at the corral and started toward the back and stopped dead in his tracks when he thought he heard something but soon walked on. At the back of the livery Luke stopped, and as he reached for the handle the sound came again and this time Luke had heard enough to know it was the sound of someone crying.

His ears followed the sound until his eyes focused on

an old wagon bed that was upside down with the under-carriage removed. Luke slowly walked toward it. "You better come out," he said.

All of a sudden the crying stopped, and an eerie quietness took its place. "You better come out," Luke said again, "And you better do it now."

"Don't shoot," a sobbing voice whined. "I give up. Here . . . here's my gun."

A pistol flew from under the wagon and moments later hands appeared, followed by a long, thin body of a boy. His shirt was ripped from the right shoulder to the elbow and both knees of his worn pants had been shabbily patched. He had big, round, dark eyes, weathered skin and a full shock of black hair that curled below the brim of his old hat. "Don't shoot—I give up."

"Who gives up?" Luke asked.

"Billy Logan."

"Where's you brothers, Billy?"

"I don't know. The last time I saw Sid he was ridin' from the alley, and I ain't seen Kirk since the shootin' started."

Luke motioned up the street with his gun barrel and said, "Move out."

But before Billy Logan could react to the command a rifle roared from inside the livery and at the same time a loud, painful groan came from up high. Luke spun with his eyes cast upward to see a man grabbing for the loft door with one hand while struggling to raise a pistol with the other. Dropping down to one knee Luke fanned two quick rounds and both found their target, but it was a waste of lead because the rifle shot had already done the job. The man pulled off a misguided shot into a pile of old lumber, then tumbled head first from the loft door, hitting the ground with so much force that his right boot came off.

Billy Logan gasped hard for air and said, "You wanted to know where Kirk was; well, now you know . . . that's him there."

"Right where he needs to be," Luke replied. Then directing the prisoner through the back door of the livery, Luke found Elam lying flat on his back, rifle in hand.

"That rascal was fixin' to throw down on you, Luke. I heard all the shootin' across the way, then a bit later I seen 'im climb up the ladder in a big huff. But after puttin' two and two together I figured he was up to no good. It was just luck that he stopped where I could get a shot through that crack yonder." Then looking over he asked, "Is that one of 'em there?"

"Yep. He's the last one—the other two's dead."

"Sid's dead, too?" the boy blurted.

"He sure is, and I can't think of one good reason why I shouldn't shoot you," Luke answered. "But we'll let the judge take care of you."

"I ain't done nothing," Billy yelped. "I ain't robbed nobody and for sure I ain't shot nobody either. You ain't got nothing on me."

"I wouldn't lock 'im up," Elam broke in. "I'd shoot 'im, Luke. And you're making a big mistake if you don't." Elam raised his rifle. "Hell, step aside and I'll kill 'im."

"No, he's right, Elam. He ain't been charged with anything that I know of, but I do think I will lock 'im up for a few days just because he rode in here with 'em this morning knowing what they were going to do."

Luke locked Billy in a jail cell and then he made his way toward the doctor's office to let Carl know Billy had been captured and Sid and Kirk were both dead.

As he was crossing the street a stranger rode up on a big bay horse, "Raymond Logan ain't going to like what's happened here this morning," he said in a low gravelly voice.

Luke looked up, "I don't really give a darn if Raymond likes it or not, and if you see 'im I'd surely be obliged if you'd tell 'im that I said so."

"Just giving you fair warning, mister. I've known Raymond Logan and them two boys of his for a number of years and I know what they're apt to do when they hear you've killed their kin."

Luke slowly lowered his hand to where it came to rest on the butt of his six-gun. "Did you ride in with 'em this morning?"

Surprised by the question and seeing Luke's hand go down the stranger's body stiffened. "No, no," he said nervously, "I've been down Ballinger way and am just passin' through on my way north."

"Then I won't keep you any longer."

The stranger sat looking down at Luke for a moment, then spurred his horse and rode on.

Luke watched the stranger until he had ridden out of sight, then continued to the doctor's office. When he got there he was met at the door by a somber looking Dorothy Fillmore and without any words said, Luke knew that Carl Padgett had died. His life had been stamped out by the Logan brothers, one of whom still lived.

Chapter Nine

Luke walked out of the hotel, stopped at the edge of the boardwalk, and leaned his shoulder against one of the support poles, reaching up to push back his hat. He looked up and down the busy street.

For the past few days he had noticed more smiles on the faces of the townfolk, but he did not know if it was because of the extremely fine weather or the fact they no longer had to deal with the Logans.

Across the way a loud voice called out and Paul Fillmore threw up his hand, "Good morning, Sheriff." Luke returned the greeting with a sweeping wave.

It had been a long and tiresome ten days since the shoot-out with the Logans had taken place. The dead had long been buried. And as of midday yesterday the town of Sweetwater had a new sheriff, a tall, wide-shouldered man by the name of Willy Wells. He had lived in Sweetwater for most of his life and was a man the whole town knew and respected. He was the youngest son of Joe and Mattie Wells, two hard-working people who had moved to Sweetwater as a newly-married couple back when the town first sprang up. But just three years back, Joe had succumbed to a high fever and died.

Mattie on the other hand still lived in the little white house at the edge of town, but once again her heart ached over the loss of a loved one. This time the pain was felt over the loss of her brother, the late Sheriff, Carl Padgett.

Elam was still bedding down in the stall at the livery stable. But he had been getting about a little more the past day or two, and was now taking his meals in the café where Mrs. Clara had taken somewhat of a shine to him. No matter what time Elam arrived, be it day or night, there was always a slice of apple pie waiting.

Luke stepped from the boardwalk and weaved his way between a passing buckboard and then two men on horseback as he crossed to the jail. When he entered he found the new sheriff sweeping the floor. "Mornin' Willy," Luke said.

"Mornin' back to you," said Willy. Then leaning the broom against the wall he asked, "You 'bout ready for some coffee?"

"Yes sir, I am. But before we go I'm going to let Billy out." Taking the keys from the peg, Luke stepped to the cell. "Billy," he called out in a loud, harsh voice.

"I'm going to let you out this morning, but before I do I want to say something and I want you to listen because it might be your last chance to get your life right."

Billy Logan swung his legs over the side and pushed up from the bunk.

"Over the past few weeks you've seen your brothers die—all of 'em—and you're lucky that I didn't kill you when you came out from under that wagon bed. To this day I don't understand why I didn't, but I didn't. And you can believe me when I say you're even luckier that Elam Langtry didn't kill you. But no matter why you're still alive, you are, and the good part is you're young . . . you've got your whole life ahead of you. Don't waste it by ending up like your brothers." Luke wanted to say more, to somehow make Billy understand there was a better way, but realizing his words were falling on deaf ears he unlatched the cell door and swung it open.

The boy stood looking at Luke for a long time then, slapping on his old hat, he walked out without saying a word.

"You think you've seen the last of 'im?" Willy asked.

"Hard to say," Luke answered, hanging the keys back on the peg. "I hope so, but you never know."

They crossed to the café and entered to find Elam already sitting at a table. He spoke over the rim of a coffee cup as they walked in. "I didn't think you fellers were ever going to show so I went ahead and ordered coffee."

"How you feeling?" Luke asked.

"Some better," Elam answered, "Still awful sore, but better."

Luke pulled up a chair and sat down, then leaning his Winchester against the wall, he turned back and said "I just let Billy Logan out of jail."

Elam looked over, "I sure hope you know what you're doing." Then shaking his head he added, "That boy's just like his brothers, I'm tellin' you, Luke. They're ever' last one cut out of the same piece of bad cloth."

"You're probably right, Elam. But we had nothing to hold 'im on."

"Hold 'im!" Elam blurted. "The way I see it you shouldn't have been holdin' 'im in the first place. You should have shot 'im dead when you had the chance."

"What will it be, gents?" Clara asked, walking up.

"I'll just have some coffee," Luke answered.

Turning her attention across the table she asked, "And you, Sheriff."

Willy smiled at the new title. "I'll have the same, Mrs. Clara, and I'd take a piece of your fine apple pie, too, if you've got any left."

"Just took one out of the oven."

Hearing the news Luke spoke up, "In that case I'll have a piece too."

She stood for a moment looking down at Elam with a big smile on her face awaiting word. "Well?"

"Okay," he said, "I'll have one, too."

"Three slices of pie and coffee coming up."

After she had gone Elam looked over. "Saw the Doc in here a bit ago and he said I should be ready to ride by the end of the week. I told 'im I needed to be ridin' now. He said I could try if I wanted to, but he didn't think my leg would let me do it."

"We'll wait," Luke cut in. "No need getting started and having to turn back. It's going to be a long enough ride as it is."

"You can go on if you want to, Luke. I know you

want to be home with your family. I'll catch up along the trail somewhere or see you back in Rising Star."

Just hearing the word *home* flooded Luke's mind with a thousand memories. He thought of his beloved Loraine and precious Jack Elam, and how wonderful it would be to see them again. He thought of Cork and Punkin Brown and Slim Fathree. Even an image of the stern, wrinkled face of Mrs. Bitters was brought on by the simple word *home.*

A long, lonely sigh fell from his lips, then looking over at Elam he said, "I wouldn't think of leaving you here by yourself. When I ride you'll be with me."

The men finished their pie and coffee, and Luke walked with Elam to the livery. From time to time they would slow down to have a look in a window or at something particular that one of the two had seen. Twice they rested on a bench along the boardwalk.

When they finally got back to the livery, the big man met them. "It's good to see you back," he said with a laugh. "I thought for sure you had drug out, so I was fixin' to rent out your room to somebody else."

Elam bowed up as best he could on a bad leg, "With all that whistling around here, wouldn't nobody want it. You've even got my old horse wantin' to move out."

The two men gave a playful laugh and took each others' hands. "Speaking of your old horse," Stine Baker said, "I reset the iron on his feet. And I put a new set on the mouse-colored horse. When you fellers get ready to head out, they're ready to go."

Luke gave a nod of thanks, "Looks like we'll be staying on three or four more days at least."

"Talkin' 'bout the mouse-colored horse," Baker said, "I sure do like 'im." Then motioning with his hand he added, "Tell you what I'd do. I'd trade you any two there in that lot for 'im."

"Don't let 'im talk you into nothing, Luke," Elam said. "He tried the same thing with me for that old dun of mine."

"That's a fine offer," Luke said with a smile, "It sure is, but I reckon I better keep 'im. If I got home and didn't have that old horse my wife would probably run me off."

At Luke's last statement, Stine Baker let go with a belly laugh and had to wipe the tears of laughter from his eyes with his sleeve. "In that case, Luke, I'd say you better keep 'im."

With little to do the joshing went on for the better part of an hour. Baker would say something to Elam, who would kick something back, and both men would laugh. Luke sat on a wagon in the shade of the barn content just to listen.

Suddenly the midday stillness came alive with the sound of horses at a gallop. Luke looked west to see five men coming fast and when they got to the jail they drew up.

"I don't like the looks of that," Elam said.

"I don't either," Luke replied. Walking toward the street, he looked more closely and when he recognized two of the men he turned back to Elam. "I don't know for sure, but I'd say that's Raymond Logan."

"What makes you say that?" Elam questioned.

"Because I've seen two of 'em—that fellow there on the big bay is the man I talked to the day of the shootin' . . . the one who warned me that Raymond would be coming when he heard 'bout it. That other one dragging up the rear is the very same Billy Logan that I let out of jail just this morning."

"He ain't had time—" Elam started.

"He ain't had time to go anywhere," Luke cut in, "not even out to the farm. I figure this bunch was maybe ridin' in from Lubbock and Billy just happened onto 'em along the way."

The man who seemed to be the leader stepped clumsily to the ground, handed his reins up to another, and labored up the steps to the jail. He stood less than six feet, with slouching shoulders and a thick, round body.

"Luke, if you don't mind I'd be obliged if you'd get my rifle," Elam said. "I left it back yonder in the stall." He flipped the strap from over the hammer of his Colt.

"Mr. Baker," Luke called out while turning for the door, "you better get to cover."

"I got me a shotgun just inside," Baker said as he widened his stride.

"You better get it," Luke called out. "But we don't want any shootin' unless they force our hand."

"Unless they force our hand—" Elam half shouted. "Heck, Luke that's what they're here for. They didn't ride all that way to tell us what fine looking gentlemen we are—they're here to kill us." Then after a pause he said, "I'm gettin' too old for this kind of livin'."

When Luke returned, he handed Elam his Winchester. "You get over there behind those barrels." He heard a bridge break and looked around to see Baker sliding two shells into his shotgun.

The lead man was coming from the jail with Willy Wells following close behind. "If you start any trouble I'll lock you up," Luke heard Willy say. The man snorted, and mounted his horse, then gouging him hard with both spurs he led the men at a hard gallop toward the livery where he brought his horse to a sliding stop. "Looking for a killer by the name of Ludd. You him?"

"Who's asking?"

The man swiped his beard with an open hand. "Name's Logan . . . Raymond Logan, and I hear tell you've killed four of my nephews for no reason."

"Yes, sir, I can't deny that it was at my hand that Pots, Leonard, Sid and Kirk all stopped breathing, but they were not killed for no reason. They were killers— cold-blooded killers and thieves, and that's a fact."

"Let me kill 'im, Paw," the one dressed in black said.

"Just hold up, Toby, there's plenty of time for that."

"If I was you I'd listen to my paw, Boy, 'cause if you as much as flinch I'm going to blow you in half."

He smiled. "If you see me flinch you're already too late."

"You better watch out, Uncle Raymond," Billy called out. "There's an old army scout around here someplace and he's the one who back-shot Kirk."

"You're a liar," Elam said while working the lever on his Winchester. "I ain't never back-shot anybody unless I had to. He was standing dead over me and I shot 'im through a gap between the boards in the loft floor."

The group of men tensed at the unexpected voice and the sound of the sliding action. They seemed even more concerned when Stine Baker stepped from behind cover and pulled both hammers back on his shotgun.

"I told you," Willy said, walking up, "If you and them boys start any trouble, Raymond, I'm going to lock up the whole bunch. Billy, we just let you out this morning and here you are back again. What are you trying to do—end up dead like your brothers?"

Billy's face grew white with the question and his lips started to tremble. He moved his mouth but no sound came out and he cast his eyes down toward the pommel.

Raymond Logan sat sizing up the men before him, his eyes switching from one to the other. It was five against four in his favor and one of them was an old man and another a blacksmith. Looking at the double-barrelled shotgun again he recounted five against five with his five sitting right out in the open. He looked down at Luke and then at Willy Wells, then slowly turned in the saddle and said, "R. W., I'm a mite dry, let's go get a little something to drink."

"But, Paw," Toby whined.

"Just shut up," Raymond snapped as he spun his horse. "You'll get your turn soon enough." Just before they reached the west end of the corral, Luke noticed Raymond looking over and saying something to the others.

"Watch 'em, Luke," Elam called out. He had barely spoken when they gouged their horses and broke into two groups—three rode north toward the back of the livery and two swung into the alley between the Sagebrush and general store.

Before the stranger on the big bay could ride clear of the corral fence, Elam pulled the trigger and the horse tumbled, sending the rider to the ground. He scrambled to his feet but with no place to hide he brought up his gun. The rifle bucked in Luke's hands and the bullet hit the man's chest so forcefully it lifted him off his feet before he fell to the ground.

Luke immediately spun around. "I'm going to the back," he called. At the back door he could hear the horses as they came around the corner of the corral. With a quick step back he kicked open the door, almost ripping it from its hinges.

Instantly bullets slapped at the doorway and splinters flew. Luke ducked and when he looked out again, Raymond Logan had stepped to the ground and taken cover behind the old wagon bed. R. W. was sliding his horse to a stop near the woodpile and just as he started to swing down, Luke pulled off a shot in Raymond's direction to force him to duck and fired at R. W. but the bullet went wide. Then working the lever as fast as he could he pulled off a second shot just as R. W. dove for cover. The bullet found its target in midair and when R. W. hit the ground he was dead.

The rifles and pistols in the front of the livery continued to bark sporadically and from time to time the shotgun roared, each time followed with less gunfire in reply.

The man behind the wagon bed had not moved since seeing his oldest son killed, but Luke knew he was there. "What's it going to be, Raymond?" Luke called out. "I'm here and you're there and I'm lookin' at you and if you move I'm going to kill you whether it's today or tomorrow. Why don't you put your hands up . . . heck, you might as well . . . you ain't got no place to go."

"That might be," Raymond finally called back. "But I'll die knowing that Toby's going to kill you. And he will, too, Ludd."

"Why don't you let me and Toby worry 'bout that."

"Worry 'bout what?" Luke heard a voice say. The words had come from somewhere to his right.

Luke looked around but unable to see anyone, he said, "Is that the boy that thinks he's fast with his gun?"

"Ain't no thinking to be done," the voice answered. "I am fast—faster than Leonard ever thought about being."

"Tell you what, Ludd," Raymond spoke from behind cover. "I'll stand up and put my pistol down here on this wagon bed and you two face off. If Toby wins I walk out of here and if you win I'll give up. How's that sound?"

"Sounds fair to me, Paw," the voice said.

For a good long bit Luke rolled the offer around in his mind. If he beat Toby he would also have to take on Raymond, because no matter what they said, neither had any intention of giving up. And how had Toby managed to get by the men out front in the first place? The shooting had stopped and Luke did not know in what condition Elam and Willy had been left—or Stine Baker either for that matter. For a while the gun battle on that side had been fierce; a lot of shots had been fired and now there were none. Had the men out front been killed? Luke leaned his rifle against the wall then reaching down he flipped the leather thong from over the hammer of his Colt and loosened it in the holster. "Okay," he called, "let's see what the boy's got. Raymond, you put your gun down and take a step back, and I'll come out."

"It's a deal," Raymond said, slowly pushing up to his feet. After laying his pistol on the wagon he took a short step back.

The rails clattered as Toby crawled over the fence. Luke glanced at Raymond who was looking in the boy's direction. From the angle Luke figured Toby had to be standing about where the fence attached to the barn.

"I'm waitin'," Toby called out.

Luke adjusted his gun, then taking a deep breath he stepped through the door.

Toby stood with his feet spread wide and his hand already positioned over the butt of his sidearm. "I've always wanted to kill me a lawman," he said. "It's too bad it wasn't me that killed Padgett. I owed that old man."

Luke took two more steps away from the door and planted his feet wide, his hand ready. "You would probably have had to shoot 'im in the back. But that's the way you Logans do things."

"I ain't shot nobody in the back," Toby sneered. "I've been looking at ever' one of 'em straight in the eyes."

"Stop your yapping and shoot 'im," Raymond blurted.

Luke locked his eyes on Toby's. "I don't know if the boy's afraid to draw or if he's trying to talk me to death."

"Why. . . ." Toby started, in the same instant dropping his hand to his six-gun.

Luke's hand flashed and the gun spoke. The bullet ripped through the warm midday air and the violent impact stopped all movement. Toby's body tensed on stiff legs, his eyes went wide to the world and his face turned white with death. Unable to raise his gun he pulled the trigger and the bullet went deep into the earth. His knees buckled and he crumbled to the ground, dead.

From the corner of the stable a rifle roared and Luke spun on his heels with his gun up to see Raymond Logan tumble over backwards. He spotted a rifle barrel sticking out between two rails of the fence at the other end of which was Elam Langtry.

"Got one pinned down over at the Sagebrush," Elam called out.

Luke turned back through the door and grabbed up his rifle. When he got to Willy, hunkered at the corner of the Sagebrush, he learned that the man inside was Billy Logan.

"Billy, you better come out," Luke said. "There's no need in you gettin' yourself killed. All the rest of 'em are dead. You can walk away from this deal if you want, too. All you have to do is come out with your hands in the air."

There was a long moment of silence and then a voice spoke from the inside. "Toby's dead? Who—who killed 'im?"

"I did," Luke answered. "But I don't want to have to kill you."

"They're all dead?"

"Yes, sir. And if your daddy is really dead you're the only Logan left."

"Uncle Raymond too?"

"Yes, sir. . . . all of 'em. You're the only one left."

"Come on out," Willy cut in. "We'll all go down to the jail and talk this thing over."

"Willy, is that you?"

But Stine Baker had made his way around to the back door and had not heard the conversation between the men. Before Willy could answer a shotgun roared and when the echo had faded the last of the Logans lay dead.

Four days later after Elam had seen Doc Fillmore for the last time, he and Luke rode out of the little town of Sweetwater leaving behind a town finally free of the choke hold of a dangerous family. For too many years the town had been ruled by fear and intimidation, as the will of the Logans had been forced on all who lived there or passed through.

The trail home was long and rough but the closer they got, the harder Luke rode. The sun was just setting on the sixth day when the two men rode to the top of the hill just west of town and Luke broke into a wide smile. They hurried down the hill at a canter but Luke slowed up to swing down when he saw Loraine and Jack Elam coming along the trail on foot. It was not until they fell into each other's arms and their lips met that Luke realized he was finally home.